About the author

Born in Cornwall, 1953, Pippa Bartolotti was a misfit at school, but a budding pianist. She blossomed at art college and became a London fashion designer of some repute.
By 1991 she had founded and managed two of her own companies, made the shift into electronics, and moved to Wales where her family would experience the joys of a country life.

Directorships of other companies followed. She took early retirement to explore different cultures and has lived in Cuba, backpacked round India, and driven a convoy of humanitarian aid from her home in Wales, across Europe to Gaza. Whilst attempting to enter Bethlehem, she was arrested by Israeli security and imprisoned.

She became leader of Wales Green Party in 2011. From early days as a Samaritan, to UK speaker for Amnesty International she has consistently campaigned to draw attention to climate change and fight for the rights of the oppressed. She currently lives in the USA.

THE SYMMETRIES
BOOK 2
BLIND SYMMETRY

Pippa Bartolotti

THE SYMMETRIES
BOOK 2
BLIND SYMMETRY

Vanguard Press

A CIP catalogue record for this title is
available from the British Library.

ISBN 978-1-80016-676-9

Vanguard Press is an imprint of
Pegasus Elliot Mackenzie Publishers Ltd.
www.pegasuspublishers.com

First Published in 2024

Vanguard Press
Sheraton House Castle Park
Cambridge England

Printed & Bound in Great Britain

Dedication

This book is dedicated to the scientists, the activists, the teachers and all those who continue to fight against the ravages of climate change.

I also dedicate this to the poor and disenfranchised of the world, the ones who suffer first and hardest. The system was never designed to support you.

Swim hard against the tide — for only dead things go with it.

Acknowledgements

With grateful thanks to two beautiful friends of mine who are yet to meet. Trudy Quaif in the US and Veronica Thomas in Wales. Thank you for your time, your suggestions, and most of all your friendship.

Chapter 1
Mother and Son

The air felt suddenly fragile, as if you could hold it in your hand and crumple it to nothing. Not crisp enough for a frost, not damp enough for rain. It was as if the North Pole had just that minute inched itself a few degrees sideways, thoughtfully tipping itself towards an overheated North America, delivering a gust of fresh Arctic air to the breathless humidity of New York City.

"Mmmmmmm. Do you feel that?" Ana adjusted her colourful scarf and looked at her son. He was facing the slight breeze, sniffing into the air like an old sea salt foretelling the weather.

"Like a gigantic air conditioner in the sky," he mused.

"Another cool atmospheric river. The jet streams are so unstable these days, it's hard to know what to expect. Could be snowing soon."

"Atmosphere, stratosphere, biosphere, interfere, persevere..." Idris was in one of his random rhyming moods.

Ana smiled patiently. Teenagers were a lore to themselves. She knew the phase would pass. Soon would be good.

"From the north by the feel of it," she ventured, hoping for a modicum of conversation.

"In July? In New York? Tough on the birds."

"Tough on everything. It probably won't last long." Ana felt more hopeful than convinced. Nobody knew what to expect anymore. It was the ice which was the trouble. It brought down power lines and burst pipes — not that there were too many left of either. One day it could be well below freezing, the next day it would be thirty degrees warmer. It could be a stifling ninety degrees in the morning, yet you would take a coat to work, just in case. North America seemed to suffer more than anywhere else. People in less wasteful countries put that down to a universal law which noted that as North America had burned the most fossil fuel, it should suffer the worst effects.

Around them, other pedestrians were noticing too. A scantily clad girl shivered and rubbed her arms as goosepimples made an unseasonal appearance. The thickly planted rows of trees in the middle of Fifth Avenue gave an elongated shudder. Their starry leaves rippled audibly in panicky commiserations with each other, their presence enabled by an equally panicky state government who grudgingly accepted that cars had to be banned and trees suddenly planted, everywhere on the planet if possible, if viable living conditions for humans were to be maintained. The United States belatedly grasped that this meant them too. New York was becoming a veritable forest. It made the humans slightly happier, but it was a struggle for the trees. Planted in ground compacted by a century of heavy traffic, each tree competed for space and nutrients in an unholy struggle for survival.

To the unpractised eye they looked like ordinary trees, but they were undernourished and unhappy. From time to time one or two had to give up the fight for life so that their neighbours could survive.

The air, so precious to life, haunted by the wilful mistakes of the past, was lately behaving very peculiarly indeed. New York in July was never for the fainthearted. High humidity. Sweaty, sticky, sickly. Humans gasping for a comforting breath of freshness. Concrete buildings blasting heat day and night, melting roads, stifling pavements — these were the usual hallmarks of the Big Apple in July, and had been for the best part of a hundred years.

Ana had been here several years ago, just before her son was born. The city stank then. It was filthy and grimy, overpopulated, under-resourced, and straining under the leash of oligarchic corruption. Economic strain defined the continual dispossession of the working classes and their surroundings. The roads were abandoned to potholes — civic buildings languished unrepaired. Politics had lacked the will, and ignored the imperative, to overcome the mounting detritus of neo-liberal kleptocracy.

But now, on this day, the dirt and odour, and maybe also the politics, had largely been taken care of. It was surprising, refreshing, maybe a little late, but all over the world there had advanced a gigantic clean up lasting the best part of fifteen years. The combustion engine had been completely outlawed, air travel was limited to one flight per person a year, and then you had to give evidence that it was an emergency. Several trillions of trees had been planted — like here in the middle of Fifth Avenue, and across the roads and avenues all over this city, every city. An electric tramway took people up and down, in and out, the pavements were wide and pretty, the stench of cars and heating units had given way to lofty trees and vertical gardens of every type. Fruit bearing, nut bearing, flowering wholesome food was virtually dripping from the balconies. The hum of city bees was comforting, and they lazily plied their pollination trade from hundreds of rooftop hives. Climate change had not gone away, and many of the subways were unsafe because of the higher water table, but cities everywhere were much nicer places to be — or so it seemed.

Ana looked at the boy. Her son. Her life companion. The light on which her love smouldered and burned, the heartbeat of her existence. He would soon be old enough to leave her. She had taught him everything she could, yet the next two years would probably see them parted. He knew it too. It was the plan — not that it was wise to make plans in these heaving times.

Years of wandering, of surviving, of laughing and crying had bound them together almost as one.

Motherhood had been her great joy. She watched as he was born. Cut the cord herself and cradled the warm wet body to her breast. Purest joy, and love, and belonging, were born too, at that moment. Bliss had been the memory, and it stayed.

He had called her Ana since he was old enough to make words. She didn't argue. Everyone knows better than to argue with a determined two-year-old. Anyway, she preferred it to Mum, or Mom, or whatever she was supposed to be called. He helped her leave her given name behind and she didn't look for it again. It was liberating. Life was liberating. He had been her liberator.

The dash of fresh breeze came, went, and came again the next day. The weather forecasters said it was a forked polar vortex. They studied their satellite images and played with their instruments and, despite all their technological breakthroughs and sensitive gadgets, were not at all sure what was happening.

"It's probably the battle between the heating atmosphere and the measures we are taking to cool it," said Ana.

"Cool, school, ridicule, overrule the mule…" Idris was definitely in one of those irritating moods.

"Iddy!" came the exasperated retort.

"OK, OK Ana." He grinned at his mother, knowing full well he was being annoying. "You're probably right. Sounds logical, the battle I mean. Nothing particularly new though."

Fluctuations in weather, climate and temperature were common fare for someone his age. Disasters of one kind or another happened every day, somewhere on the planet. Reports were always from the human perspective. Flooding, fire, pestilence, thousands lost and missing, millions on the move, millions dead in heatwaves. He was used to it. They continued their walk.

Idris had been brought up in a remote Welsh valley, in the hidden meadows of Llanthony, just as his mother intended. The longhouse, almost a ruin, had been occupied by an eccentric old man who befriended her in the late stage of pregnancy. He had made a room for her, shown her how to grow food, how to adapt to a gentler life, how one planet living was possible, sensible, fulfilling, beautiful.

She would pull at the beets, the parsnip and the carrots, brush the soil lovingly from their roots, and know that here was the memory of all which had passed before. Of every leaf which had fallen, every molecule of compost, every worm, of every fungal mycelium, there was a trace of the universal history stored, intact, a line of unbroken fertility, a living relic of the stardust from which everything on this blue planet originated. The organic, perfect, nourishing catalyst of life. Microscopic, overlooked, yet here, everywhere, waiting to be worked and reworked into ever more generations of plants and animals. Linking the primeval soup of creation to the evolution of amazing future creatures, design unknown, yet always recognisable, just as the lineage of ancient dinosaurs passed down through the millennia to modern birds.

The wonderous soil which nourished them had become part of them. Her son, who had known little else, was as rooted in this place as the parsnips and the old man before him. Yes, he was of this place. The atoms in his body were composed of the food he ate, which in turn were composed of the nutrients in the soil from which they grew. This was the sense of belonging, imbibed over a lifetime, which defined home. This was the song of the earth, the irrefutable calling when you leave.

But leave they had. When he was twelve, Ana decided it was time for Idris to embark upon a broader education. He had a good grasp of history, of philosophy, of anthropology. He was, of course, numerate and literate, but whilst the world of other countries and cities he knew in theory, he had yet to experience the true flavour of their culture. It was not enough to read or hear stories. It was important to smell, to taste, to interact, to laugh and to cry, to feel the heartbeat of other ways of life.

Gently and sensitively the woman and the boy had meandered across Europe. They loved the quiet pastoral roads, the tiny European villages eking out their food supplies as they waited for the rain, any rain, and relaxed in the lazy bays of the Mediterranean — the lazy, hazy last days of the old life where the fish still swam even as the great inland sea warmed beyond their capacity to evolve.

They visited the old cities as the waters lapped steadily at their grand institutions of monarchy, oligarchy and kleptocracy. The wandering had taken three years. A tentative root of friendship had developed in some places, less so in others, but Ana felt there were many places her son could return to if he so wished, if they were still there.

Now he was fifteen years old, and they had very little time left together. The Americas were too big and too diverse to cover in a matter of months, so, hitching a ride on a transatlantic sailing boat, they opted for New York, the Big Apple, the city of survivors, of innovators, of repurposed spaces and generous, frightened, people.

Chapter 2
New York

The skyline hadn't changed a lot since the coronavirus pandemic, some twenty years before, but everything else had. The eternally mutating zoonotic virus had exhibited more intelligence than its human host. Immunologists all over the world worked in a constant round of catch-up, with the disease forever a few steps ahead. Herd immunity was unacceptable politically, but the viruses were not looking for votes. They could have been looking for laughs. Hollow laughs. For no virus intentionally kills its hosts, yet this new breed was happily skipping from one species to another and back again with only the slightest genetic modification to its killer blueprint.

The balance of play would always be in the virus's favour, and suddenly governments were wondering if there would be enough healthy people left to pay the taxes, pay into the pension schemes, buy the cars, the gadgets and all the stupid things which kept a debt-based economy in business.

New York, proud hub of the world's international commerce, was the hardest hit.

Isolation, illness and death did not buy consumer goods, but it bought space. It bought time to reflect, time to understand what had gone wrong, and time to imagine how to put it right.

In the cruel times, when they realised that the first virus was mutating faster than they could immunise against it, New Yorkers found themselves sitting in a nervous waiting room in the game of who dies next. But the hiatus in everyday activity gave them time. People of all ages and groups began to understand that they might have the power to change the paradigm, to change the prophesy. Desolation and ruin were not inevitable. They asked the questions 'who' and 'how'. They asked who they themselves were, and how they should best be living in their part of planet. The answers came, and they kept the faith, and followed the questions to their logical conclusion. There was little choice anyway. The writing would have been on the wall had the wall not already been washed away.

Ana and Idris walked through the city in curious wonder. It was not the bright and shiny centre of commerce of its capitalist heyday. In truth it was rather tawdry, with unrepaired broken windows on every level and flaking paintwork, but at ground level, every nook, every cranny revealed something interesting. They could not always tell what it was, but it looked to them as if invention sprang out of every crack in the walls. Change had been happening all over Europe, especially in the cities, but here in New York there was a certain magic.

The Green Dream, as they called it, was started in the centre of the city, in the places where fossil-fuelled traffic had already been banned to give more space to pedestrians trying to stop the spread of disease. One disaster had been paving the way for the next since the Industrial Age, but here was the hypothetical line in the sand, and disaster started to pave the way for remedy. Thus, disease prevention was paving the way for climate rescue. It was the wrong way round of course.

The trees had grown rapidly and were now almost thirty feet tall. They wafted and wavered their shadows across the cracks in the pavements and roads.

"London planes," said Ana examining the flaky bark.

"Why London?" asked Idris.

"Good with pollution and rubbish land. It's been used in cities for a long time. It deserves better."

Idris 'um-ed' in acknowledgement as he walked round a nearby specimen, musing. "Trees, bees, sneeze. So many trees. Suddenly. All at once. Traffic to trees. Smog to soil. Grime to green. Sneeze to bees…"

"Yes Iddy," said his mother, examining her slender ability to be patient and wondering just how long this particular phase would last. "They need more trees than people to keep the city air clean and shaded. More than double the number I would say."

"We all need more than two trees then. How many did we plant in Wales?"

"I didn't count after the first few. Hundreds probably. And we nurtured and protected many more."

They sat down on a massive section of wood deposited on a grassy verge. Six people could sit on it comfortably. On the side was carved in large capital letters 'IT TAKES TWO MINUTES TO GROW THIS MUCH WOOD IN NEW YORK STATE'.

"Decent," said Idris when he had read it.

"The thing is not to cut them down," said a merry voice from behind.

Ana and Idris turned round abruptly. Sitting behind them and facing in the opposite direction was a bespectacled woman with glossy dark skin and outrageously bright lipstick. She inched round to face them better, tossing her silver braids aside.

The amply proportioned woman stretched out her arms and embraced the sky. "Welcome to my beautiful city." And she beamed an instantly likable toothy smile showing an insanely large gap between her two front teeth.

"I overheard you talking, I hope you don't mind. I can help you with a bit of backstory if you like."

Ana nodded generously and urged her to talk more. Idris looked decidedly sceptical, as a fifteen-year-old should.

"Of course it started with the trees. It had to. Every day you plant a tree it is twenty years too late." And she chuckled hugely at her own joke even though she had probably told it a hundred times before, and rushed on regardless.

"So, we just started doing it. It was a kind of resistance and empowerment. It wasn't very scientific in the beginning. People just started planting where they could — a patch here, a corner there. We planted anything, everything, but the thing was that we took entire responsibility for the trees we planted. We protected them, watered them, fed them, talked to them. When they got bigger some of us actually hugged them. Yes!" And she fell back roaring a deep, gurgling, contagious laugh.

"I think the hugging did more for the people than the trees, but who knows. Who am I to judge? Lots of people do it. They go out in the evening to chat to their trees. It's beautiful!" And she clapped her knees in mirth. "I do it!"

"Maybe the trees deserve a hug for actually saving our lives." Idris carefully entered the conversation.

"Maybe you are right. I can't argue with that. But there are also the people who have fought to save the lives of trees."

"Self-preservation," said Idris looking distantly up the road in a deliberately distracted posture.

"Quite true," smiled the woman amicably. "Did you know that old wood has closer rings than new wood?" And without waiting for an answer she proceeded in an enthusiastic gush of words. "It's because a couple of hundred years ago, when there was less carbon dioxide in the atmosphere, growth was slower, the tree rings were closer together. It's said that it wouldn't be possible to make another Stradivarius instrument today because the wood growing now grows too fast. Anyway," she jostled herself away from reflection, "the thing is not to cut them down at all. Not for a hundred years at least."

Her speech was hurried, enthusiastic, as if there was so much to say and too little time in which to say it. "Aoko. I'm Aoko. Really appropriate as it means an 'evergreen blue tree'. I think my mother saw one as she was giving birth to me, or so the story goes. African. African American. It's our culture. We have our own distinct culture. All the groups do. We are colourful and diverse. What's your name?" And she finally paused for breath.

Ana and Idris introduced themselves, agreed on a local tour and Aoko launched into her next breathless flurry of information.

"You see, we survivors had discovered that at heart, after the pandemic — not that it's entirely over of course — we wanted to care more for each other than ourselves, and the ripples of caring spread wider, so we began to think collectively. Although a chronic amount of biodiversity has already been lost, yet barely missed because it initially seemed that humans did not need it, the beautiful fact dawned that every little bird and every fluttering butterfly teetering on the brink of extinction, every little insect, and bug and bee, needed the people for survival. It did not matter that they were not needed in a direct and obvious sense — although in many cases they were — what mattered was that we needed people to pay attention to their existence. All we humans had to do was stop killing them."

Aoko continued apace. Ana wondered if Aoko had the capacity for circular breathing whilst she talked. Maybe she played the digeridoo in her spare time, such was her ability to breathe without pausing, adding copious streams of asides in every sentence she uttered.

"The trees are of course amazing. It had to start with them — for lots of reasons. The city wasn't moving very fast with de-carbonisation measures. Then came London — London frightened us all — London was the catalyst — we have our floods here too of course — more often nowadays of course — but instead of depressing us it motivates us. Lots of different groups trying out different things. Look at this!" And as her voice rose in child-like excitement she pointed with irrepressible gusto to the facade of a nearby building which seemed to have about fifty oblong fish tanks of murky green water, spaced like windows and running up from street level. The dark green water was gently moving.

"Algae!" announced Aoko with tangible pride. "We've been working on it as a really effective carbon dioxide absorber and oxygen producer — just look at that! When it's bloomed we dry it, and it is the most effective composting material we have — even better than humanure — or so I'm told. All it needs to grow is sunlight, water and a stable temperature. The buildings we already have, so we make them work. Solar collectors, wind collectors, algae farms and a bit further on we have vertical food farms."

Ana and Idris studied the buildings with respect and appreciation. Human ingenuity forced into the technological development it should have completed in 1980, instead of leaving it to the veritable last minute, the actual eve of destruction, when the riders of the apocalypse had already saddled up.

"I've heard that you've also been doing interesting things with water," said Ana.

"Oh yes, the water. Storage. Irrigation. Look over here! We run it through the streets in summer to help with cooling — and because it makes a happy sound. It improves humidity — though I doubt we can change the entire world climate with these few little streams. It might help though — actually of course it helps more if everyone is working to the same ends — I mean all over the world — at least wherever there are still actual people!" She chuckled that particularly mesmeric Caribbean chuckle which emanates from deep in the stomach and vibrates its way up to the throat and ends with a huge smile.

"Everything, unless it is completely exceptional — and I can't think of anything which is right now — has to have at least two uses. One can be purely aesthetic, of course. There has to be beauty, and quiet. We were making so much noise before that we couldn't find the answer to our problems. Now the quiet gives us room to think, and that's a beautiful thing."

The water rippled happily through the streets as Aoko described. Three little children were floating paper boats along it. This was Fifth Avenue, a transformed Fifth Avenue. A happy place of trees and water and humans helping each other along. Gone were the endless snarls of yellow cabs and worried people rushing about trapped in an anxious state of being, too hot or too cold, too rich or too poor. The new magical Fifth Avenue had people old and young shopping for fresh food grown locally in one of the roof gardens or vertical farms, or pavement forests. All the parks and indeed any viable space with sunlight and shelter had been given over to gardens of one sort or another. The rainwater was collected in underground cisterns partitioned off from defunct subway systems. It was primarily used for irrigation, but it also had a dampening effect on temperature in the streets and buildings above. The stored water kept the summers cooler and the winters warmer — all good for people and plants. Grey water such as shower and washing water was pumped to the roof gardens or used to augment the vegetation growing below, where it was cleaned and fed back through the system in a series of gently sloping gullies. When they reached the bottom of any given slope, the water which had not been used was pumped up through an ingenious system of pipes and cupped wheels, a wonderous sight on its own.

27

"Take a look at this!" exclaimed Aoko, wheeling round and pointing excitedly to something which looked like a shrubbery — as if she was seeing it for the first time. "You see, we have what you might call affinity groups pooling knowledge and resources to innovate and improve what we are doing. These compost beds were designed by a group of mostly Mohawk and Seneca residents — they still carry ancestral knowledge of what grows best in this area — and when the city government stopped trying to stop us, we didn't have time to dig up every road and pavement — and anyway the soil underneath was sterile to the point of being useless — so they invented these nutrient bags which are crop specific."

She raptured over the forest garden filled with trees and bushes and corn, and all manner of edibles growing. It was not at all like the neat rows of vegetables Ana had been taught to grow back in Wales. Bags of different sizes and nutritional composition were put together in a modular system, so parts could be replenished when necessary.

"You've got a huge mish-mash of things in here," Ana countered, peering into the shady depths of one such container. There were small trees for shade and shelter, bushes bearing fruit, salad crops, root vegetables and herbs, all jostling together and looking vibrant and lush.

Aoko carried on in full sail. "Of course it's up to every group to do what they like — after all, they are the ones tending — and it works out that if each group decide what to grow — based on their preferences — there is always enough variety across the area to please us all. A sort of naturally self-selecting system. We put it down to community interaction — you know, comparing notes — this grows well here, but that grows well there, sort of thing. That's what we do. We talk. We share. We do. We get on and do — we have to — no time to waste. All very good for planning, and the soul you know. We have to feed the soul as well as the body — very important — that's the side effect of working with nature, and good air, and exercise. Essential for the body and every other function, spiritual. Very important." And she finally ran out of breath.

A group of colourfully dressed people cantered by. All flounces and frills and reds and yellows and chattering smiles. They stopped in front of Ana and did a little dance.

"It's not just trees and plants you know," chuckled Aoko regaining her breath in a nanosecond, her bosom rippling with vaguely supressed mirth. "It's art and culture and fun too. That's the Mexicans — a merry bunch. We don't divide ourselves by knowledge and labour, or geography or gender or anything really. But we do acknowledge the big part culture has to play. You know, the roots of people, their lore, their stories, their generational substance."

"They're in national dress," exclaimed Idris in poorly contained wonder. He had finally caught on to what was really happening in the city.

It wasn't just about food and energy. It was about people and happiness and continuity and love.

"Yes! It's Friday!" enthused Aoko. "If they want to, nationality groups have a national dress day. It doesn't have to be a Friday. The Tibetans started it because the exiles always had a national dress day — to remind them of their country, and their roots and their shared sense of family. It was such a good idea that other groups wanted to do it. You see, we don't travel a lot physically, but we do travel a lot mentally. I mean to say that we are always learning, sharing, inventing new ways to do things, or reinventing useful old ways. We are cross-fertilising if you like. Many of us will never go back to wherever 'home' was, so we recreate parts of 'home' wherever we are!" And she pressed her hands together in unabashed happiness.

"Wonderful," said Ana. "This was always a vibrant city, but in the wrong way. Now it seems to have become vibrant in the right way."

Idris, his interest piqued, had a question. "What happens if a person doesn't like the work they are given?"

Aoko gave her lavish smile and slapped her thigh. "Nobody gets given work! They just try things out until they find the thing which interests them most. We need people with a passion! We haven't time for anything run-of-the-mill. Already some of our most fertile soil in the south of Manhattan is being salinated. We're in a massive hurry. We don't need innovators carrying soil — unless they want to of course — but that doesn't really happen — I mean they do sometimes, you know, for the exercise."

"And who pays them?"

This seemed to be a familiar question, and Aoko nodded knowingly as she hurried through the answer. "Now let's think what a person really needs. What do you need?"

"Well, food, and clothes, and friends, and drink…" He tailed off, already getting a feeling for where this was going.

"Exactly!" exclaimed Aoko clapping her chubby black hands together with gusto. "What if all that was just given to you — and more! What then?"

Idris had hardly been brought up in a materialistic way, but he clearly thought there was a place for wanting more.

"I don't know. What if you need a new something to replace an old something, like a bike, or a tap, or something?"

Aoko finally looked serious, but she didn't slow down. Her breathless enthusiasm started once again to run away from her as the words and ideas tumbled out. "There is no new. The natural systems cannot afford the cost of extracting materials and the associated pollution — no matter how we minimise it — not for maybe two hundred years. New York is an experiment. We are learning to manage without new. We maintain, we reuse, we recycle and upcycle. We understand the lethal cost of convenience, the imperative of repair. The world was once too keen on buying new — and not a thought given to the energy and the resources and the pollution needed to produce it. If you mine a twentieth century rubbish dump you will probably find everything you need in an everyday sense. You will find things you can make work again — things to repurpose, upcycle, a life with purpose, constructing good, constructing something from a discarded item which was once worth nothing. It is contagious. People find they have skills, ideas, purpose."

"What about the scientists and the inventors?" asked Ana.

"They are a special case. We can't let innovation be held back." She looked at them both in turn, a more serious tone to her voice. "If you want new, then you'll need to study hard. Innovation is essential." And she cast her eye back to the algae windows soaring up the side of a nearby building.

"But we dream of more than this — much more. We dream of less struggle, we dream of nano-particle applications in biomedical, optics and electronics, of better medicines, smart machines and frictionless transport. We have so many dreams."

Ana wondered if the gardens were really her area of expertise. Maybe this warm and friendly woman was a scientist.

"Let me introduce you to a gentleman who can tell you more." And Aoko bustled beamingly up to a tall skinny shred of a man in a battered straw hat.

"This is Red. He is one of the original architects of our Forest City."

Chapter 3
Red

Red bowed majestically, removing his hat with one hand and crumpling it almost to destruction with the other. "Aoko is always generous. I am but a humble cog in the great wheel of this city."

"It is indeed a great wheel," said Ana extending her hand. She introduced Idris.

The tall man immediately, quietly, applied himself to Idris, bending his long thin frame imperceptibly forwards, his quiet voice tinged with direct insistence. "Where is your main interest amongst these marvels of human ingenuity?" And he opened his arms wide.

Idris shrank a little. He hadn't expected a question to be directed at him in particular. He mostly left conversation to his mother who considered it one of the higher arts.

"Let's go over there and sit out of this cool draft." And Red pointed to a small cafe with tables and chairs huddled amongst the riotous growth of a city garden.

Indeed, that cool air had reappeared without notice. Ana pulled her colourfully painted scarf around her shoulders like a shawl and sat down in a sheltered corner of bay trees and aromatic herbs. The warm smell of sweet rosemary mingled with bay and thyme to almost intoxicate a person, and she breathed in deeply, sighing in olfactory satisfaction.

They ordered some locally grown tea.

"We don't get so many visitors since long distance travel became unacceptable, so it is our pleasure to explain to you what we are doing here, and to exchange information, and to learn from outside our own practices."

Idris, who had clearly been thinking hard about the question he had just been asked, gave voice to what was in his mind. "I guess I'm most interested in where you started. I mean what you were thinking when you embarked upon the changes."

Red smiled gently, leaning into Idris just a little, scrunching the wrinkly corners of his eyes into a quizzical gaze. He took off his hat once again, crumpled it into slightly more destruction, ran his fingers through his thinning grey hair and replaced the mangled hat. "This, is a very good question."

The tea arrived in a clatter of mismatched crockery.

"Honey and thyme," whispered Ana as she sipped it. "Reminds me of Hania." She looked at Idris. "Reminds me of your father. This was the first drink we took together."

Idris had never met his father, and the years had passed beyond longing to a slight nervousness at the thought of meeting him. He yearned to know him yet was afraid of knowing him. Their cultures were so different, their histories had never converged. In a form of subconscious compensation, he tended to study most men he came into contact with as a potential father. It was a kind of practice, a dress rehearsal for the real thing. And the real thing was less than eighteen months away if everything went to plan.

In this frame of mind Idris subconsciously returned the quizzical look Red was giving him. Red, always on the lookout for young talent and fresh ideas. Idris on the lookout for a father figure to fill the gap between the aged Welshman he had grown up with, and the blind Arab he was yet to meet.

"What were we thinking?" mused Red aloud, picking up a thread of the conversation. "In the beginning, after London flooded irrecoverably, and the scope of the calamity was filtering in, we were thinking we must leave New York. Large flooding events until then had been somewhat in the abstract and mostly rural. New York is on very low ground, like London. We were afraid. The tipping points were galloping towards us. Of course the flooding event had been predicted long before, but nevertheless the entire world system was wobbling in shock. Economically, socially, environmentally, the ripples from London caused everyone to question everything anew. There seemed to be no safe place — at least no place where safety was guaranteed, so some left, some stayed. The city was divided between the fatalists — who could sit back and let things happen to them, and the activists who were burning to do something about the situation.

"The city government was stuck in the old ways, scrambling hard to maintain the status quo. No funding for this new idea, no funding for that one, but still giving tax breaks and subsidies to the oil and beef barons. It was unfathomable. No laws allowing vegetable gardens on sidewalks, no provision for water storage. No concept of a change which could be fast enough to fire the imagination, no model to change thinking faster than the climate. For a time, it was chaos. The rules were outdated, but enforceable. Even those enforcing the antiquated statutes could see where the old idea of future was going — to hell in a handcart."

Red sat back in the chair. He liked telling stories. He was a historian after all, and it was still incredible to him that his history, the history of his own recent lifetime, was a story worth telling.

He continued, checking his audience was still with him. "So, the collapsing economy pretty much ground to a halt, and the emphasis of daily life began to change. There was no rush to the office when there wasn't a useful job to go to. Importantly it was realised that most jobs were absolutely pointless in the new scheme of things.

"To illustrate what I mean," he interrupted himself to make quite sure his new audience were fully understanding. "What was the point in trying to sell new kitchen units, when the real worry was not how swanky your kitchen might be, but whether you had enough food to make it worth having a kitchen in the first place! No, there was urgent, new and necessary work to be done, not the old pointless work. New Yorkers needed to claw back their valuable time to help nurture the blossoming new infrastructure projects. Job vacancies petered away in favour of the new informal, survival economy which needed plastic kitchens a whole lot less than it needed the food to go in them — so we got to work. Real sustainable work."

Ana and Idris were aware that most people knew what climate change would actually do, from a theoretical point of view at least. Many had mentally prepared themselves for what precautions they might take to stay alive, though theory and practice rarely converged when acute action was needed.

Red continued. "In the city there were already beekeepers. Monarch butterflies lived here even in 2020! Roof gardens, experimenters and seed gatherers were tucked in all around the city. Had been for years. Importantly there was a surprising collective of individuals determined to make positive change, and to force that change. It was almost half the city, and we made the ultimate bargain — to risk everything by staying here, to share everything, and to learn to love, properly, unreservedly and wholly. Only in this way would we survive. The spiritual side of our ethos cannot be underestimated. It's a kind of innovative, spiritual practicality."

"But these changes have only taken fifteen years?" said Ana.

"Yes, pretty fast really. But so much trial and error. So much error!" Red took off his hat and wrung it half to death as he warmed more closely to his subject. "There was no uniformity of thought. We were as many differing thoughts as there were people. I guess the most measurable breakthrough was with the trees. Small collectives or individuals lifted a few paviours to plant trees here and there. They called it guerrilla gardening. No plan. More of a protest really. The authorities usually dug them up the next day. We were getting nowhere fast. Frustration was building."

Ana could perfectly understand the situation. Scientists had been fighting their own governments for years. "Was there a true beginning? Can you pinpoint the beginning of organised resistance?"

"I guess," said Red, casting his mind back to what seemed several lifetimes ago. "I guess the beginnings of any organised fight-back came with the volunteers. You know, the usual suspects. The retired, the environmentalists. Then the architects and historians. Local committees began to form and drag out street maps, rainfall charts, soil tests and calculators. They formed strategies based on little more than best guess, and their calculations were brilliant because they knew that even if there was only a one in a thousand chance of their children experiencing terrible suffering, they must act immediately. To stop further uncontrollable climate change and their equally devastating cousin, zoonotic disease, they knew that they needed a viable plan to decarbonise, revitalise, and to forge meaningful co-existence with every other living thing, and they had to plan to develop more, because non-human diversity was being fatally diminished.

"Then the would-be gardeners started taking over incomplete building sites, and planting trees in the rubble. Believe me, under all this, New York is ninety-nine per cent horrific, infertile, toxic rubble. Then bands of neighbours came down out of their high rise and protected the trees, quietly, determinedly, and the magic started. It was incredible. You had to be there to understand, to feel an absolute sea change in people's attitudes and behaviour. The city could pull up a couple of trees here and there, but they could not pull up a few thousand — especially if those few thousand were protected by a few thousand residents."

He shook his head with glee at the memory. A wide smile acknowledging the memory. The impossible had happened and in his head he was reliving it with gusto.

"Of course, there were heavy political arguments. Of course, property developers were furious. Of course, businesses which relied on heavy transport were incandescent with rage. Of course, politics as usual was completely out of the window. We were one people with one aim. All the petty differences were seen for what they were. Even voting was seen as a false dichotomy. It took more than one leap of faith to persuade the developers that there would soon be no insurance available for the buildings, no profit left to squeeze out of the city. Business could still make a modest income, but they had to recalibrate their business models. Heavy transport could no longer come through the city. Goods had to be transported from the periphery by alternate means — horses, electric, hydrogen. It was messy."

As if to illustrate the thought, a colourfully bedecked rickshaw clattered by. Flags waving merrily. Cyclist shouting a greeting.

Ana mused on the picture developing in her mind. She had seen this sort of change in the European cities they had visited, but not on such a vast scale.

"Why is this so successful here in New York? I've seen similar efforts in Milan and Madrid, and Berlin too, but here it seems so... so... incredible. The scale I mean. It's like everyone is with the programme."

Red saw the insightful light in her eyes, the sense of recognition that in this place something different was indeed taking place.

"It seems," he said, "that everyone is indeed with the programme. But that is not altogether true. There is plenty of resistance, some of it unpleasant, but the positive outlives the negative. Quiet argument and relentless campaigning is necessary. New Yorkers had long been dwelling under the cloud that their pollution levels were higher than average, that their health was suffering, that their contribution to climate change was exorbitant, yet they did not think they had the power to change a thing. Always the economy came first. Always the elections came in to artificially divide us. Always the treadmill, the rat race, the clamouring for more money, more stuff.

"You know." And he stopped to smile conspiratorially in the direction of Idris. "We forgot about all that nonsense surprisingly quickly as our sense of emergency rose. It was all insubstantial you see — the old economy I mean. Neo-liberalism, capitalism, call it what you will. It didn't make anyone happy, except maybe the super-rich, but we stopped thinking about them long ago."

Idris nodded. He had been protected from the rat race and its coercive bedfellow, consumerism, but he knew about it all right. He had been tempted by the idea of flash cars he had seen in magazines — what lad would not have been. But thanks to the nature of his upbringing, underlined by the cataclysmic events of pandemics, sea level rise and vicious storms, his thoughts moved in a more beneficial direction and, after a while, he started to concern himself with reflections on where he would fit into the interesting world forming around him.

Red leaned forward conspiratorially, as if sharing a precious secret. "You know, this area, hundreds of years ago, was once a hunting and fishing paradise for several tribes of Native Americans. There were deer, moose, cougar and racoon and so much more. The rivers were full of salmon and seal and whales. But just imagine, the most prevalent animals in this area by 2020 were the cockroach and the rat — and of course the humans."

He shook his head in past remembered despair. "In order to go forwards, we had to look back. I am a historian. I did not dream that my studies of American Indian culture would be fundamental in planning the future. But the architects and engineers dug me out from under the dust of my books and questioned me night and day with an urgency which took me by surprise." He smiled to himself, his eyes shining in remembrance. "And I thought I was only good for the odd lecture in which half the class fell asleep."

Ana, who was fond of history herself, could easily see the link. Life in the Welsh longhouse she had stayed in with the old man had continued much as it had done since the hand-hewn stone walls were first fashioned some hundreds of years before. She and Idris had lived the history of their land in every mouth of food, every chock of wood. It had been the almost sustainable lifestyle she craved. Almost, because they still used the old jeep which carried them up the hill. Almost, because they bought luxuries like toilet paper and soap. But it was a decent enough life, for the times, for the beginning years of a child.

Mother and son had walked through the splendid medieval ruins of Llanthony Priory on sunny afternoons, relishing the high ecclesiastical arches and poetic

43

shadows, imagining the old farms dotted around, the monks calmly working the fertile soil on the valley floor. A pastoral existence seemed the essence of tranquillity. Simple, quiet and contemplative, they read much in the long winter evenings, especially history, but this quiet life was never enough to satisfy her, not for long. She stayed for the boy, her beautiful olive-skinned son, to ride out the squalor and dissolution of the coastal towns as the fabric of twenty-first century existence quite literally decomposed, and the inevitable upheaval of humanity as it came face to face with its own folly.

"History," she mused aloud, almost drunk with the warm fragrances in the air around her, "teaches us all we need to know, but we have to teach ourselves how to apply it."

"Indeed," said Red, liking her attitude. "It is the application of knowledge which is the tricky part, not the gaining of it. Knowledge is not the same as wisdom.

"For example." And once again he stopped himself to explain what he meant — half a lifetime in the classroom did not easily leave his mannerisms. "It was commonly thought that the indigenous nations would know what to grow and how to grow it. They did — two hundred years ago! What to grow on poisoned rubble in the middle of a concrete jungle — even if the ancestral land is on the same latitude and longitude, is quite another matter. Yes, history told us what was grown here, but history could not tell us what would grow here in the present. It needed scientists, historians, biologists and botanists to find a way to grow successfully. Even the famous Three Sisters needed more than a bit of rubble on which to thrive."

"Three Sisters?" Ana and Idris looked up enquiringly.

"Yes, it's a local thing," Red replied, forever keen to share a bit of historical knowledge. "Maybe five thousand years ago the Mohawk discovered that corn, beans and squash, when grown together, protected and helped each other. The corn became a trellis for the beans, and the spreading squash protected the roots of both. They have long been referred to as the Three Sisters. It's a form of companion planting which we use to great effect all over the city." He beamed at them, satisfied that he was sharing yet more knowledge.

"But we digress. By bringing together so many disciplines, so many people, all in one place, we obviously encountered differences of opinion. Yes, we needed the multi-disciplinary approach to solving our problems as fast as possible, but we were worse than children, wasting precious time arguing over which way would be best. Many of us had deep knowledge of our specialist areas, and the danger was that this could blind us to the wider picture."

"So," said Idris, reverting back to his original question. "Why is it all so successful here in New York?"

Red crinkled the corners of his eyes knowingly, aware that he was taking a roundabout route to get to the answer. He loved to extol the holistic virtues of his learning.

"Indigenous wisdom. In so many ways, indigenous wisdom was, and continues to be, the most important asset we have. We were lucky. We had indigenous Americans within our community who had kept tight to the wisdom of their ancestors and guarded it carefully. They knew before anyone how destructive humanity had become. They tried to tell us decades before, but few would listen.

"You see, indigenous wisdom is more encompassing and profound than all the sciences, the arts and the humanities put together. It embraces gratitude, love, respect, social cohesion, and a deep sense of responsibility. Scientists tend to block these emotions in the name of objectivity and look for universal principles that can be replicated anywhere. Indigenous wisdom is different. It is the amassing of accumulated observations, trials, and errors over countless generations. It is the sum total of the successes and failures of generations of people living in one particular place. Over the centuries this knowledge, passed down from generation to generation, was critical for survival. It is the very best tool we have."

Ana nodded. "It is what we learned living close to the land in Wales. The interconnectedness of all things, the web of relationships with all animals and plants, with the air, the water, the microbes in the soil, the sunlight, everything. It became part of us, and we learned to replenish and nurture all these things as an intrinsic part of our continued survival."

Red nodded enthusiastically in agreement. "Yes, it is the element of reciprocity, of responsibility, which is missing in contemporary science, and society in general. We took. We never gave. We like to think our communities here are on the way to correcting that. The question of learning, and unlearning is ongoing, and our place in this world has to be relearned if we are to survive as a species."

The cold draught which had caused the leaves on the trees to shrink a little, was lessening. Survival in these unpredictable times was not guaranteed. A layer of anxiety underpinned every thought and action. Tomorrow might not be as kind as today. A prolonged frost could mean hunger for many, and there were worse things than that.

Red's penetrating gaze alighted once more on Idris. "We have workshops most days if you are interested in learning more detail. How long will you be staying?"

Idris looked at Ana, unsure of how involved in this vast community of activists he should get. "We are staying about a month. It depends on when our boat leaves for the return journey."

"Then look out for the boards all over town with the timetables of activity. We welcome you, your input, and your thoughts. We would also be most grateful if you would carry our knowledge back to your homeland. We can only gain collectively from interchange of knowledge and expertise. The toughest problems are whole world problems. They need whole world solutions."

A colourful array of Asians drifted past. Bright coloured saris and tinkling bells and laughing faces. It was Friday, after all.

Chapter 4
Honesty

Ana and Idris were staying in two large rooms in a low-rise apartment block on East Twenty-Third. It was modestly furnished with sofa beds, a small table and two wooden chairs. Oddly the bigger room sported a huge crystal chandelier — dust settling on the cobwebs, a remnant from another time. They guessed the chandelier was not needed anywhere else, so it stayed where it was. It might have had as many as thirty light bulbs at one time. Today it had one. It looked hilarious. They speculated that there was no black market for chandeliers in a time when the main priority was food, but it was a fine object just the same. The cooking and bathroom facilities were communal. It was more like student accommodation, which made sense as most visitors were students of one form or another.

"Well, we're here to learn," said Ana. "And there seem to be a surprising number of opportunities in which to do so. What do you fancy doing tomorrow?"

Idris was already making plans. "I noticed there was a forward planning session in the morning just round the corner. What they are doing now is pretty cool, but I'd like to know what they are planning next. It could be exciting."

Ana smiled, pleased that he was enthused with the activities of this city reborn. She wanted him to be part of the new cultures of respect, and responsibility. It would be tough, but it would be his world.

For her part Ana decided to volunteer in the gardens, to give her labour in exchange for the food and lodgings they had been offered. In a transactional economy it always felt better to give more than you received, and a couple of weeks hard labour would do her good. She was anxious to get her hands into rich loamy soil again, her direct line to the planet and all things living.

The first morning of work was on one of the low-rise roof gardens. The structure had been deemed strong enough to carry several tons of wet soil. Around the edge of the building were small fruit trees on cordons to act as windbreaks, themselves protected on the windward side by hardy hedging. Within the cordons of fruit trees were various bags of composted soil being prepared for planting. The work was varied. She could choose between carrying heavy buckets of soil, kneeling to plant beans or herbs, or whatever was due to be planted out that day, or just tidying up. In this way no one was overburdened, and everyone could change jobs at any time. It became a loose rota, with people palling up for conversation, or just working quietly, deep in thought. The sun shone brightly, with just a cloud or two overhead, and the breeze made working pleasant enough.

Her work buddy became a robust older woman, full of energy and knowledge, enthusiastically shoving her be-ringed fingers into the soil as she planted the hardy herbs of rosemary and lavender for harvest the following year.

Her name was Lydia. "We never really know what the next season will deal us," she yawled in her strong Brooklyn accent. "So we plant hardy up here where there is good sunlight but big draughts. We lose a few, we win a few, we keep going because we keep going."

"And you are learning all the time," added Ana.

"Learning? For what? I sometimes think. No pattern to the weather already. Today's trial can be tomorrow's tragedy. We learn for today only. Tomorrow? What tomorrow?" And she cast her rhetorical questions to the air with a roll of her eyes and a shrug of her shoulders.

Ana stared at her. Unused to this kind of attitude.

"Tragedy. That's all we got. We keep busy to keep from thinking about tragedy. It's going to end in tragedy. It has to. No good worrying about it. Humans. I tell you. Humans. We expanded to every corner of the planet, destroying whatever we could make money out of. The land and the trees, the animals, insects, everything. We had the ability to take ourselves over the edge, and we used it." She shook her head and rested her grubby hands on the knees of a pair of trousers which looked rather expensive.

Lydia looked at Ana's serious face and shrugged her shoulders more forcibly. "Don't tell me about it. I spent a lifetime worrying already. Where did it get me? It got me a whole pile of knowledge so that I could know for sure we are finished. It's a shame. Six thousand years of hopes and dreams. Enough technological potential to achieve harmony with each other and the habitat. What do we do with it? Make a war or something. Completely useless. History, fine arts, music and philosophy — all down the Suwannee. We melted the ice, the permafrost, we lifted sea levels and demolished the infrastructure of our own existence. Look at us already! Tomorrow we down tools and finish the evacuation of Lower Manhattan. What a bunch of losers. Let's get some tea."

With that she grunted uncertainly to her feet and steered Ana over to the trestle table where someone was pouring tea and offering biscuits.

Ana couldn't be more interested. "So tell me, Lydia…"

Lydia interjected, "Call me Lyd. Everyone does. It's short for 'put a lid on it', because I don't know when to shut up." She nudged Ana who was looking particularly serious. "It's a joke. It doesn't cost to laugh. OK it's a bad joke." And she had a hearty laugh at her own expense.

A more peculiar mixture of doom and jollity Ana had yet to meet. "So tell me, what's going on in Lower Manhattan?"

Lydia sipped happily at her tea, then dunked a sweet oatmeal biscuit in it. "Lower Manhattan? Flood zone. It's low. Maybe that's why they call it Lower Manhattan." She laughed a kind of extrovert 'Ha!' "I don't know. It's a

Munsee name. They said the hickory trees round there made good bows. Yeh, that would have been nice. They should have left the hickory trees. Manahahtaan means 'the place where we get bows'. They should have left the trees... They should have left a lot of things..." And she took a satisfying slurp of tea.

Ana resisted the temptation to agree with Lydia about the more desolate thoughts she harboured, mainly because it was too big a thought. Yes, they would lose the cities, the coastlines; yes there would be even more hardship and shortages and death, but also there would be good change. Like here in New York, like Madrid and Barcelona, where people's minds moved from thinking about self, to thinking about their neighbours. Where collectivism was shoving selfishness aside. Where pooling resources and abandoning profit was the credible, if not the only, way to survive.

By mid-afternoon they had planted hundreds of young plants and Ana had done her fair share of lifting. It was good work. Hearty work. Her cheeks were pink, her body felt good and her nails were broken. She had rarely been happier.

Over the final cup of herb tea, a few of them sat round to discuss the plan for the morrow. It seemed that they were to retrieve from Lower Manhattan all which was useful, or beautiful, and of course portable. The upper floors would be good for a few years yet, but the task was to abandon the lower floors and drill mooring rings into the pillars and walls. The plan had been rehearsed before in similar situations around the island. Electricians and plumbers would take what they could safely salvage whilst leaving services to the upper floors intact if possible. Plans had already been brought up to prepare for pedestrian bridges to run from building to building, and any materials on site which would aid this undertaking were to be labelled and carried to an upper floor. It was a huge logistical undertaking. Carts were to be brought to certain locations to carry what could be retrieved, and people were stationed at various points inland to help with unloading. There were plenty of empty apartments and offices, so room for everything and everyone.

Ana, for a moment, contemplated living here, in one of the spacious, deserted offices with a view over the Hudson. She liked the company. She liked their forthright approach to problems. But in truth there was not enough honest land to make her happy, and in any case their next travel goal would be Levanta, and Hania, the father of her child. It was a promised reunion.

Food was served that evening in the communal kitchen of the low-rise apartment they temporarily lived in. It was a tasty mixture of salad and pulses, fruit and fresh bread. About twenty assorted visitors and residents scattered round the tables and chairs. Idris appeared, fresh faced from his day in planning and a long walk by the river's edge.

"How was it?" Ana asked.

"Pretty good," came the reply as he flopped down in a soft chair.

"And…" prodded Ana, eager to hear some detail.

"Well. We ate well, we walked about, we talked and we listened to all kinds of interesting stuff."

Ana groaned. Teenagers could be so infuriating.

"And…"

He grinned. It was great fun teasing her. "The general gist was to work out how we can give this place back to nature. It was really for my generation as the task will take decades. Obviously we have to prevent extinction. We have to grow people as well as plants and trees. We have to stop unravelling ourselves and the society we are creating whilst letting nature find its own way. Pretty exciting."

It clearly was, Idris had enthusiastically wriggled himself almost to the floor in his excitement at retelling the day. He propped himself back up again.

"Ana, you'll like this. We did an exercise on planning the ideal Forest City. Forget what we have here. It might just be a staging point and New Yorkers might not be able to manage long term. This ideal city would have no more than a hundred and thirty thousand people in it. Botanists and landscape architects would select the species of plants. It seems four hundred different species would be about right to achieve biodiversity, but there would need to be more than seven hundred million of them, plus two hundred thousand trees. That's near to the figure we talked about yesterday. More than two trees for every person."

He paused for breath, his teenage enthusiasm still working hard even at the end of the day.

"Shrubs, bushes, green roofs, vertical gardens, planned demolitions. It's about achieving the perfect balance between green areas and people."

Others in the room began to listen to him, and he felt mildly uncomfortable.

"Of course, there are those who say that all cities are a bad idea." It was a resonant voice from the other side of the room.

"This one is," came another voice.

"Well its home to us," said another. "We choose to try and make it work because it's home. Our family are here, our friends. Maybe it won't work out. Maybe it will. We have to try."

There was a general murmuring of consent. It was clear that the way ahead was going to be difficult — both physically and mentally.

"Cities are a natural progression," said Ana. "We may start in tents and villages. We cluster together to share resources, labour, security, and the tent village grows bigger, and eventually becomes a town or city."

The deep voice from across the room revealed himself. Tanned skin and long black hair, his nose large and slightly hooked, reminiscent of the Native American warriors whose proud and poignant features adorned the history books of this continent.

"Cities like this one are not sustainable, never were, never could be." He leaned forward, an earnest look on his face, his wide shoulders hunched as if protecting his subject. "It is all artificial. The water is pumped, it used to be cleaned, it used to be treated with chlorine, fluoride, orthophosphate, sodium hydroxide, and ultraviolet light to make it safe to drink. I do not know if people still do this work, but I do know that already you boil and filter your drinking water."

He continued, an honest earnestness in his face. "If the power drops you cannot get water to the top of the buildings. And the sewers. There are hundreds of miles of sewers. You do not have enough people to maintain them. The entire infrastructure of every city will fail one day, little by little the deterioration will manifest itself, then you will have to rework the city existence until catastrophic failure."

"Do you not think there is maybe a middle way which can still be sustainable?" asked Ana.

The man half rose and introduced himself in modest greeting. His deep voice boomed across the room even when lowered. "I am Jake, by the way. My given name is Dakotah, Friend of Friends."

Ana introduced herself and Idris. She reciprocated by telling the room in general that Idris was unusually both a

Welsh name and an Arabic name. It meant interpreter, studious, prophet.

Jake nodded and smiled. Anxious to maintain the flow of his subject, his resonant voice took back control of the room. "Is there a middle way? This is what we are applying ourselves to. My people no longer live in tents and follow the buffalo like the old days, because there are no buffalo. We cannot live in harmony with nature until nature is restored. We were truly sustainable two hundred years ago, but in country or town we are now together with you, now, you, the impoverished city dwellers, thinking it through, working on survival. There is a middle way, a progressive and more gentle way. Plans were drawn up decades ago. Plans gathering dust. The dust has to grow thicker before we are ready."

He continued, elbows on knees, using his broad hands to describe his seriousness. "We cannot build. We cannot cut a tree. We cannot use cement. We can only quarry in a limited way. No, this is not the generation to build. We are the generation to survive, and to plan. We are the ones who can lay the foundations, but we cannot build on them. We live with what we have, and it is our destiny to watch it slowly decay."

"It must be documented," said Ana, completely understanding the concept of the fascinating American Indian. "It must be well documented so that the mistakes can be evident, and the decay can be recorded, and the lessons learned so the future doesn't have to repeat the folly of the past."

The serious newcomer paused, as if wondering how best to state the obvious. "We have repeated the documented follies of the past over and over. From Mesopotamia onwards we know that meddling with the earth's systems brings downfall."

Ana was unbowed. "Those matters of failure were fairly local. People could easily move on and leave the disaster area. What is different now is that the disasters are global. There is nowhere left to run. We have to make what we have work. It is an imperative. If anything, the people are running here, to escape hunger. They are coming here, to a city. It is the reverse of history."

He allowed her the point. "Because it is the reverse of history, it is not automatically going to be a success."

She couldn't help herself. This man, this Jake Dakotah, was drawing her in. He was attractive in that earnest, guileless way which hit a certain spot in her anatomy. Her defences were alternately dropping and rebuilding. She could feel her own pulse in her heart. It had been a long time since she had been attracted to another man, and it was becoming rather too quickly clear to her that this one, by his every movement, was stirring her sexuality. 'Rare enough,' she mused to herself, for attractions of this sort were to her very rare. There had been Idris's father, a lone troubled man with a head full of shrapnel and heart full of ideas. Yes, Hania had been an unusual man. Now this Jake Dakotah, maybe he was a loner too, strong enough to bear a solitary existence, even in a crowd, and indisputably full of good ideas.

He leaned into her, and she wondered if the feeling was mutual. "Yes, document the decay. But also document the new beginnings. I am only here in the city for a short time, to observe, and share, and work. Something completely different is happening out in the desert."

Chapter 5
Jake Dakotah

The frisson between them was palpable. Tiny shivers ran up and down Ana's arms and spine and she allowed herself pleasurable thoughts of being closer to this large, spontaneous eruption of a man.

They had been talking across a room full of people, but now it was as if they were only talking to each other. The magic had started.

"Tell us about the desert," Ana asked. She was very interested in the desert, but she was also very interested in hearing him speak, watching him speak. Listening to the timbre of his voice. Watching those large hands move in swooping gestures and expand his meaning. Something inside her was reaching out to something inside him. He was nothing if not persuasive. Voluble, energetic, down-to-earth, she was transfixed by his train of thought as it moved from one discipline to another in excited explanation. From geology to chemistry, physics, climatology and of course his own morphology, he careered across the purpose of his work — to green the deserts in the shortest possible time.

"Many people are working themselves almost to death in the central latitudes. The deserts have been growing faster than we can turn them back. It is a terrible battle. We have been trying to attract rain, reinvigorate the soil, turn the direction of extinctions round. We do this because we too will be extinct if the deserts grow at this unstoppable rate. Fewer people we might be, but hunger is just one drought away, one storm away. We call the people working the deserts Generation Restoration. They are our only hope for the future."

Ana knew there was work happening all over the world to turn back the deserts. Africa, India, Europe, China. She had the impression it was mostly tree planting, rewilding, and the breaking up of monocultures, but rather than speak, she wanted to listen to this fascinating man, Jake Dakotah. She wanted to make love to him every bit as she wanted to listen. In times of uncertainty few people bothered with courtship, and in any case the chance of a pregnancy was always welcome. With the stress and uncertainty, the effect of the plastics, the disease, the vaccines created to overcome them, plus ongoing human displacement as storms and tides encroached on the most populous parts of the land, pregnancy had been the last thing on most people's minds — until it was noticed by its absence.

Jake Dakotah looked to be in his mid-forties, worn rugged by the sun and wind, formed muscular by physical work and dedication to his craft. His train of thought halted for a moment as he realised this woman was affecting him strangely. Like his ancestors he paid attention to his spiritual side, and here was a being whose presence pulled at his inner core. He would make time to see her again. He would not deny his innermost calling.

"Nature is regenerative," he said softly as if imparting a great secret. "But we, all of us, have not allowed natural regeneration to take place. We have been killing the land, the water, the animals, even the air. This we know. How to put these wrongs right, in time, before it's all lost. That is our quest."

The room full of people finished eating and drew themselves closer to him. Listening intently. News of what was being achieved in the desert was always important. Vital. Even before their love affair had begun, Ana knew that he was a gift she would always have to share.

"Restoring a landscape as large and as degraded as the Mid Lats sounds like science fiction. The soil has been farmed to death. It has no nutrients left. There is drought. Grass fires spread for miles. Sometimes hundreds of miles. The wind dries the land and whips what's left of the topsoil away, and the rain has almost stopped completely. We could deal with this when it was just Utah and Arizona, but quickly the dry tide has run up the south-east and we are losing Ohio and Pennsylvania. Wildfires are everywhere and we have no choice but to let them run."

There was a low gasp. Clearly those present had not known how bad things away from the city had become. It felt as though the sea lapped at them from one side and the desert from the other. A siege of self-inflicted disaster at every turn.

Jake Dakotah continued, aware that he didn't want to spread alarm, but at the same time not wanting to lull them into a false sense of security. Telling the truth was important. Denying the truth had brought this catastrophe upon them.

"We have been working fast. Working down the rivers and rivulets. We work south and north. North to maximise what has not been lost. South to recover what has. Do you want to know how we're doing it?"

Eager nods surrounded him.

"Lots of low tech. Nothing fancy. Planting trees on hilltops to contain water run-off. Surrounding each and every one of them with smooth river stones to condense the dew. The moisture runs off and thus nourishes them. The choice of tree and mix of species is very important. We've been terracing the steeper slopes — mostly by hand with picks and shovels so as to disturb as little ground as possible; retaining all the moisture we can; adding organic material in trenches, any organic waste, from wherever we can get it — human, animal, plant, anything. We are trying to reinvigorate the broken web of microscopic fungi which should run under the land. We want wild and grazing animals to be free, but we have to control them in the short term or they will eat the small trees and plants which are essential to restoration. The animals are hungry too, and they will be free to roam again when the balance is right.

We feed them, but we must corral them, and keep their numbers manageable for the next few years. There are hundreds of people looking after the wild animals in as near to their natural surrounding as we can contrive. We are growing animal diversity, and we will be reintroducing many species over time, but right now it has to stay manageable in size."

He spread his huge hands. "I like to think of soil as the womb, and vegetation as the midwife. The child is a healthy and diverse landscape."

"Is it working?" asked Idris, enthralled by this new rehearsal father figure who had crept upon the scene. "I mean, are you seeing results? Good ones?"

Jake Dakotah smiled. "It is very soon, but yes, if we can just reform a really big area, I believe it will work. There is no better mechanism for removing carbon dioxide from the atmosphere than nature. But right now she needs help. Essentially, we are trying to build a wetter landscape. We are seeing good results in the rivers already. Since industrial farming was stopped, and industry in general ground to a halt of its own accord, the pollutants simply stopped getting in the way of health. The fish are returning in bigger numbers every year. We didn't need to do anything at all. We just needed to stop poisoning them. Together with our efforts on land we will eventually rehabilitate natural predators and restore a healthy balance. Water begets water. We may once again eat fish in the future, but very rarely. It will not be encouraged. It is imperative that we change our behaviour, our mindset, in order to sustain the health of the land. This is the greatest existential challenge I believe humanity has ever faced. If we get this balance of coexistence right it will be an evolutionary step for humanity as big as fire."

"So you are saying that since we discovered fire, we have only been destroying the balance of nature, but what you are doing is rebuilding nature," teased Ana.

Jake looked abashed and laughed nervously. "Well, I think we have been on this overtly destructive course for the last two or three hundred years at least." He smiled, and his eyes took the smile further, and they took his amusement and interest in her direction. It was a curious and gentle expression, humorous too. "And it's not just me out there reforming the land, there are thousands of us!"

Ana at that moment was quite happy for him to be a god. She laughed back at him. "So who was the ultimate architect?" She was almost offering him an apple.

He caught her drift. "Ah, do you mean the great architect in the sky, the one with the long grey beard?"

There were audible chuckles.

"It is possible your god was a committee, a team, an array of experts. I am none of these, just a humble morphologist happy to throw in his lot with other scientists and put his skills to work. But of one thing we must be sure. The old sedentary, agricultural way of providing food will not continue. The surviving groups of *Homo sapiens* will have to adapt to somewhere between nomadism and

66

hunter gatherer to avoid the unsustainable mistakes of the past. No more monocultures. A more active, more thoughtful life is called for. Not everyone is going to make it, but it will be a healthier, happier human who lives on through to the next generation."

The evening naturally descended into an excited question time, everyone forgetting for a moment they were all malnourished and living on the skimpiest frill of existence. Jake Dakotah answered everything in his open good-natured way. He was sorry he could not bring them better news about the food supply, for it was still too early for the desert experiment to part with any of its produce, and in any case there was barely enough to feed the working people on site.

Then the room broke into smaller groups, assimilating the information, reshuffling themselves in the grand order of common interests and burgeoning friendships.

Ana took the three steps needed to stand beside Jake Dakotah. He casually suggested they go somewhere quiet to talk. She acquiesced, and they walked down the stairs to the street. The energies which surrounded them as individuals, blended seamlessly together. They walked and they talked, all night long. When the sun rose they could be found leaning against the smooth black rock of the Manhattan Schist in the Central Park Garden, her flowing patchwork skirt, the skirt of generations into which her whole life and family were woven, covering them both as they snuggled close, talking sleepily, arms entwined, content.

The gentle sound of waking people camped out in the park drew them to the day, and the spell which had bound them to the night, gently broke.

The grass was damp and the air fresh. They rubbed each other's arms and jumped up and down to reinvigorate the circulation and wake their sloozy minds.

"Come and share my breakfast," said Ana, straightening her skirt and expertly rebinding her long dark hair into the crown of Germanic plaits which was her customary style. She made to drag his bulky figure in the direction of her apartment.

"I will, if you will afterwards come and share mine."

People were already milling around, carrying furniture and pots and assorted bundles of wire.

"Oh, I forgot. Today is the evacuation!" Ana quickened her step. "Quick, I must catch Idris, and then we eat a bit, then we go to Lower Manhattan to help clear the ground floors. It's going to flood sometime soon, and today is the day we move what we can." She looked appreciatively at his muscular frame. "We are going to need you. Come on!"

Jake Dakotah was inclined to do whatever she asked.

"Have fun?" asked Idris, stuffing the last of his breakfast into his mouth whilst swiftly drinking something they called coffee and which was actually nothing like it. Everyone could tell the difference, and no one said a word.

It was the best concealed joke in the world. The way people said 'do you want a coffee?' with a question mark over their heads and their eyebrows raised. It was of course a ludicrous charade. The legendary taste for morning coffee in America had become one of the best jokes ever. It was roast barley. There was no coffee.

Jake and Ana smiled back at him. Idris winked. It was almost imperceptible. Ana grinned. Her son was definitely of age. He was making everything easy for her. It was his nature, and maybe his upbringing. He dashed off some words about going to help out with the installation of the stuff coming up from the lower land, and was gone. It made Ana happy to see he was finding independent purpose here.

Hundreds of people toiled up and down the sticky streets all day, a thankless high humidity day. The sort of day when pushing plants into bags of soil on the airy roof of a low-rise building would be an absolute blessing.

Exhausted by heat and work, many chose to break up the day with an occasional swim in the Hudson River, where the water lapped up to the rails of what used to be Rockefeller Park, where the cool water revived flagging energy. By the time the sun was sinking into the mist of the west, carts laden with food for the workers trundled down the avenue. Fresh bread, oils and salads quenched their every nutritional need, and their tastebuds stayed happy too, for the cooks knew what they were doing. It was not enough to just take care of the health of these people, these survivors, it was important that they found enjoyment in the food too.

They ate enough and lay out on the road to dry. Some of them started to sing. It was a searching lament. Ana caught some of the words, 'Let the children sing again, Let the grass grow high, Let the people live again, Under the starlit sky...' She had heard it somewhere before. On the road out of London, round the evening fires where traveller refugees from the city joined together to discover a new life, a better life. It was odd to hear it again three and a half thousand miles of water away.

A steady drip of refugees from south of the island joined them as they walked back to their lodgings. Over the bridges came more. Large parts of Newark were not going to survive the next storm. It was anyone's guess when that might be, but wisdom lay in forethought and anticipation. A once in a hundred-year storm happened every year. No one argued the truth of that anymore.

"They won't get further than Manhattan now," said Jake sorrowfully eyeing the trickle of humanity passing before them. "I hear all the surroundings islands have now deemed themselves full and are fortifying. They are protecting themselves with bows and arrows."

"I heard that too. It seems we are only ever one step from savagery. Just one small step."

"Which is why we need to work so hard with the idea of community, socialism, it doesn't matter what you call it. Helping others to help others is a full-time job. That's why the forever workshops, the planning, the work. It's got to be about sharing for the common need, and we have to reinforce it every hour of every day or it will be as you say, savagery, a bloodbath."

Ana looked deeply into Jake's twinkling eyes. Hooded they were, dark, broody, but honest. He looked directly back at her, softening, a smile twitching at the corners of his mouth.

"Shall we sleep together tonight?" suggested Ana.

He chuckled, a deep rumbling coming up from his stomach. Pressed against his chest she could feel the vibration pass through her own ribs and the echo of his laugh almost became hers. "I was going to ask you the same thing!" They stood, her arms on his, his on hers. It felt like home.

"Let's not mess up our respective kitchen people again. You eat at yours and I'll eat at mine, then I'll walk over and find you."

Chapter 6
The Gardens

"If all the trees and plants died, we would die. If all the animals and fish died, we would die, but if all the humans died everything would probably get a whole lot better. You can bet your bottom dollar on the plants and critters not giving a damn either way." Lydia pushed her hands firmly into the soil with a degree of finality. "Not a single damn."

She heaved herself to her feet. "This is the meaning of life for me now. Can you believe it used to be diamonds, and furs and designer bags?"

Ana didn't like to say so, but she did believe it, not least because Lydia was still wearing some of those diamonds as she spoke.

"Yeah. I was shallow enough. Rich enough. Stoopid enough." She threw her hands in the air. "Oy Vey! I couldn't see what was under my nose until it wasn't there to see any more."

Ana got up from where she had been planting seedlings beside her and carried back a tray of young bean plants.

"What changed you?"

"I used to like gardening. I would say 'dig up that plant over there and move it here'. That was my kind of gardening." She chuckled, moving the back of one composty hand across her forehead. "But I did develop some knowledge of a sort. Unfortunately it wasn't concerning the stuff you can eat."

She laughed at herself. "So what changed me? My son died of the virus. We don't even know which one. That changed me. It changed me a lot. I looked for all sorts of reasons why. I needed to blame someone, something. Not very generous of me I know, but I was grieving. He was my only child.

"Then I found out about how the forests were being destroyed, about zoonotic disease. I knew all about climate change. Everyone did. But I was rich. Climate change was for the poor. Why should I worry about what I ate, or what car I drove, or how hot I kept the greenhouse, or how many trips to anywhere I took. It wasn't my problem. The politicians could sort it out." She gave a wry smile. "Yes I knew they were all corrupt, but I didn't think that was my problem either. Turns out it was all my problem. I lost my beautiful son. I lost my husband. It was suddenly my problem."

Ana, nodded. She knew there had been many people like Lydia, most of them probably had an even worse attitude.

"Yup. I thought being rich would protect me. Except it didn't. Did you hear the story about heaven and hell?"

Ana shook her head in mild amusement. Lydia was in full stream and would have told the story even if she said had heard it. Her rich Brooklyn accent lent a beguiling mixture of absurdity and gravitas to everything she said. Ana loved listening to this mad old Jewish woman up here on top of the city, where the cool breeze blew and the green leaves rustled.

"In hell, the people sit at huge tables groaning under the weight of the most delicious food you could ever imagine. You could eat whatever you liked. As much of it as you liked, for as long as you liked. The catch was that you had to eat with the utensils provided, and they were forks and spoons ten feet long. Everyone is starving because they can't get any food into their mouths.

"In heaven they have the same tables with the same food and the same utensils, but no one is starving because they are all busy feeding each other. That's about it really. That story was my road to Damascus, and I can't even remember where I heard it." And she shoved her hands deep into the loamy soil again. "If we don't feed each other we will all starve. The big ole' penny in my big ole' head finally dropped. You could have heard it a mile away."

"I was in London you know," ventured Ana, "on the night of the flood."

Lydia paused with her arms straight and her hands thrust deep in the soil. She had heard a great deal in her life, and although listening wasn't her strongest point, she was listening now.

"It was horrific. I just wanted to run. Maybe I should have stayed to help like you, but it was too awful. Bodies, stinking mud — oh the smell of it haunts me still, I was in advertising, a job I disliked... I wanted open spaces, trees and meadows, so I stayed to do a bit of clearing up and left as soon as I could. I'd like to say I left everything behind, but truth to say I had nothing to leave behind."

"Where did you go?" asked Lydia, all interest visible by her absolute lack of motion.

"Well, I had an approximate plan to hide myself in the wilds of Wales. At least that was the approximate plan until I met Hania."

"A man. I knew it. Always a man gets in the way of what a woman wants to do. You fight it a few times and in the end you give up and make some sort of compromise with yourself, which usually ends up with you not doing the very thing you always wanted to do. I have had three husbands. Don't tell me about it." And her hands came flying out of the soil to join her shoulders in emphatic remembrance.

Ana knew what Lydia was trying to say. But things had changed dramatically for everyone since London. The future was not going to be the same as the past. The man-woman relationship, in the teetering balance since the dawn of Christianity, was finally tipping decisively.

"Well not exactly. Perhaps yes and no," responded Ana. "I did not have a good idea of what I wanted to do, only what I did not want to do. I did not want to settle down, to get married. I did not know the first thing about children and didn't want to know either. My dreamy ideas as a young woman were more fields of buttercups than scholarly achievement.

"But along the busy road of displaced people, frightened people, I met a group of doctors, intent on giving all the travellers healthcare. They were really beautiful people. Their hospital had been more or less washed away and they were heading for a new base. They travelled in an ambulance and were some of the happiest people I've known. That's how I met Idris's father. He was travelling with them."

Lydia was very much in the market for a new story. Storytelling was part of her life. She used to visit older friends who couldn't get around too well because of illness or age, and who would listen to her everyday stories as part of sorely needed entertainment devices, so she tried to coax a little more from Ana. "So was he a doctor?"

"No! Hania had come over from what used to be called Palestine to be assessed for possible surgery in a British hospital. The hospitals in the Gaza strip at the time were short of basic equipment. With the bombings and the despicable siege, together with the pandemic, there was no chance of his life being saved unless he came to Britain. A bomb had exploded close to him. He had some shrapnel lodged in his brain, and the fear was that it was unstable and affecting his eyesight. They had not completed the investigations when the hospital in London was half washed away. He had nowhere to go, they liked him, there was no rule book, so they took him with them. Honestly

Lydia, he was such an interesting man, I was completely bowled over by his charm and his philosophy."

"Palestinian, eh?" laughed Lydia. "Did you know I'm Jewish?"

Ana hardly needed a clue to work that one out.

Lydia nodded to herself. "Trouble and strife all over the Middle East. Arabs, Jews, politics, polarisation. I never understood a word of it. No. Not even their names. I mean, Menachem. What sort of name is that? Moyshe! We used to laugh about it, my first husband and me. Everyone changing their names to become more Jewish, or less Jewish, or maybe Jewish. Thank god that's all behind us. What a waste of time that whole Zionist project was. Unbelievable!" And her eyes rolled to the sky in earnest exasperation. "Waste of life."

They did not discuss what they both knew, that the Israeli government had produced a novel vaccine to try and get ahead of the continually mutating coronavirus running round and round the planet, and had deliberately withheld it from the people whose land they had confiscated — the original inhabitants, the Palestinians. They did not discuss the unfolding generational disaster — the Abaddon.

Ana dedicated her next day to learning. It would be of little good to be here in this crucible of invention if she could not pass something useful on to others.

She chose a tour of the gardens — the ones on ground level. Every patch of green, every city square, every large junction, had been transformed. These were very busy places. Her guide for the day was Pedro, a Cuban, who had brought with him all the relearned techniques won in poverty and hunger when the collapse of the Soviet Union, now fifty years ago, severed the supply lines of staple foods and gasoline. Of course gasoline was practically outlawed now, but the suddenness with which Cuba was faced with this existential crisis caused a certain amount of panic as the country rushed to feed itself. The United States at the time was a role model in how to be a bad neighbour. Just ninety miles away from Cuba, the preferred US strategy was to punish the people for their socialism with starvation.

The history lesson thus given, Ana was treated to a whole new world of agriculture. Ploughs drawn by oxen and horses. Mules and donkeys carrying baskets of fruit and vegetables, rows upon rows of oats and sweetcorn, beets and kale, garlic and potatoes and blueberry bushes.

Ana learned that it was all about nutrition. Obviously they could only grow crops which flourished in the climate, but the choice was further pared down to nutritional values. Every so often there would be a row of huge slatted compost containers. Nothing was wasted. Not a leaf, not a petal, not a shred of human excrement. Everything was broken down and ploughed back into the soil to enrich it for the next season.

"Manhattan was not exactly overrun with parks," said Pedro. "And none of the parks were fields ready for planting. We had to tear almost everything up and start again." He grinned. "We did leave the trees, though some would say we could have made our lives a lot easier, plus made more room for food if we had taken those down."

She could see what he meant. It was difficult to dig around so many trees, but the shade was invaluable.

The tour continued. "We have about half a million people to feed here in Manhattan. That's a lot of food three times a day every day."

"Can you do it?" asked Ana.

"Probably not for long, if I'm honest."

This was the terrible truth. Climate change wasn't stopping just because humans had decided to do something about it.

"We are desperate for the desert regeneration efforts to succeed. We need to encourage people out of the city. Every space we have is filled with crops, inside and outside. We are growing mushrooms in the old subways, sprouting seed like alfalfa too, baby greens, anything which can grow in those conditions, but the race to grow food is using all the effort we have. No one is maintaining the buildings, the infrastructure, the water supply. In another thirty years all this…" He looked up to the towering skyscrapers, so long the hallmark of Manhattan. "All this, will be chronically unsafe."

"So it's a question of short-term survival then?"

"Yep. One day at a time."

"Are you hopeful?"

Pedro grinned a beautiful set of even white teeth. "Of course!" Then he looked serious. "It is the ultimate bargain — we risk everything by staying here."

The sound of unshod horses clopping along made Ana turn round. The hilarious cliché of a handsome man in shining armour, riding a white charger to rescue a damsel in distress peeked into her mind, for there was Jake Dakotah riding bareback, relaxed and easy, leading an extra horse. She laughed at the scene.

"Look what I found!" he announced as he slid down the horse's flank. "This is Frank and this is Irma." He laughed at her expression. "Don't look at me, I didn't name them."

Frank was a wide girthed gentle gelding of advanced years. His grey forehead stooped to nuzzle Jake's arm hopefully, and Jake dutifully responded with some carrot peelings. Irma on the other hand was larger and offered little more than a look of equine distain, as if she was worth more than this everyday clopping around town could offer. Maybe she longed for fields and fresh grass for, quiet though she was, there was always the need to look over the hedges and walls to check if there was anything more hopeful on the other side. One dappled, one bay, they were completely unalike, yet intelligently friendly towards each other.

"How did you know I was here?"

"In that skirt? In that scarf? With that hair? Everyone knows you are here!"

Ana looked abashed. She knew she had her own way of dressing, but often forgot quite how eccentric she could look.

Jake led the horses into the shade and offered them drink. "I'm told these two haven't had much exercise lately, so an evening ride seemed like a good idea." Then came a sudden afterthought "You do ride?"

"I can sit on a horse and pray, if that's what you mean."

They hugged, closely. She would ride if it meant being with him just a little longer.

He heaved her unceremoniously onto the smaller mount. Ana threaded her fingers through the pony's mane, smiled an uncertain smile, and together they clopped gently along the dusty remains of what was once the clamouring Broadway.

"Did you know that the earliest pathways for moving around Manhattan Island followed animal and Native American trails across difficult terrain. Broadway still follows one of these routes. We're on it now."

"Are we going anywhere in particular?" asked Ana as she fidgeted around on the blanket spread between her and her horse.

"Sort of. I thought it would be nice to ride with you, just for its own sake, and from here you can get a slightly different perspective of the city."

He looked at her sideways and gave an impish grin — as if a six foot four, broadly built, hook nosed American

Indian could possibly be confused with an imp. "I thought we might visit the Botanical Gardens in the Bronx, and you did say you wanted this to be your learning day in the gardens."

She nodded and grinned. It was clever of him to work his schedule into hers, though she did have some doubts about her ability to withstand the horse ride. The horse itself was no trouble. Placid and wide backed, Frank was surprisingly comfortable… for the short term.

He smiled back, acknowledging her thoughts.

She learned along the way that the Botanical Gardens had long been involved in the diversity of plants, animals, fungi, and habitats in the city. The politicians and the media might have tried to ignore and deny climate change, but the botanists all knew exactly what was happening.

Through the latter part of the twentieth century they raced to identify the myriad and surprisingly diverse flora which could be found in the city, one third of which they knew to be under heavy threat due to relentless urban development and changing climactic conditions. Jake wanted to look at their work and establish if anything was missing from the large restoration projects in the hinterland. He hoped to be surprised.

Ana slid inelegantly down from her horse, and staggered. It had been a ride of several miles and her legs were stiff and getting sore.

"I don't think I'll ever get my legs together again," she said as she tried to stretch herself straight.

Jake Dakotah played with that boyish sidelong look again.

"Suits me!"

Ana feigned a blow at his head.

"But I'll carry you back if you really are in trouble." And he pretended to lift her there and then.

This mixture of hilarity and thoughtfulness was most beguiling.

They tied the horses western style, and made their way into the soaring glass cathedral of ancient research for the advancement of botanical science and knowledge, the New York Botanical Gardens. Still splendid, still shining in the rosy glow of a late afternoon sun, still proud. Like a frosted wedding cake with a million encrusted diamonds it rose, layer upon layer of impossible curves and domes and fanlights, shining white and glistening.

Inside, the planting of trees and shrubs was awe-inspiring and beautiful. Floral beauty rose on every side and the quiet dignity of the people working there contributed to the feeling that this was more a living library than a glorified greenhouse. Charts and measurements were pinned close to every living thing. As they walked through the different zones, from desert to rainforest, grassland to temperate, Jake fondled leaves and stooped to gather the scent of various plants. He was in ecstasy; she was just impressed.

"Would you like to stay in the glasshouses whilst I go over to the library. They are expecting me about now."

Ana nodded graciously. She was learning more about the man than the plants.

But there was no end to her curiosity. Tucked into a side display of one of the long glass corridors she found something most interesting. It was a sample of all the edible plants which had grown in this part of the world before it was devastated by concrete. Here she lingered long.

The survival of ancient people, the Native Americans and maybe even those who came before depended entirely on what grew locally, naturally, unhindered and unhelped by modern humans. The variety of edible plants took her by surprise.

There were wild leeks, burdock greens, wild onions, beach peas and serviceberries. Foods she hadn't heard of like hen of the woods and Indian cucumber, ostrich ferns and sea rocket. All the nutrition a person could need was labelled and catalogued. Hickory nuts, black walnut, pine nuts, hazelnuts, oak acorns and beech nuts, wild rice, rose hips, persimmon, blueberries blackberries, raspberries, elderberries, cattail roots, dandelion greens, cranberries, wild strawberries… she would never remember them all. She looked round for someone who could help her with a list so that she could share all this information. Because of all the planting she had seen, little of it resembled the items before her eyes.

Then her enthusiasm plummeted. A small note at the end of the display drained her hopes. It said:

Although these edibles once provided sufficient nourishment for the humans and other animals which lived and travelled these parts hundreds of years ago, they struggle to survive in the heightened acidity and polluted ground created through rapid urban development.

Although it was warm in the glasshouse, she pulled her scarf close around her shoulders as if struck by a sudden chill. She was shaken. Her excitement at what was happening in the city had clouded her sense of reality. Of course Red, Lydia, Jake, and everyone else closely involved in growing survival crops, knew all this. That was probably some of the error Red and Lydia had talked about. They had probably tried all these things, and found they didn't work, or at least didn't work well enough. She sat on a small wooden bench to think everything through.

Modern man had destroyed and polluted everything in its path. Discovering what was recoverable was almost thankless. The city dwellers had started again, recreating the soil through whatever means they could, and the means was not, at least yet, providing the conditions for many native species.

Someone was walking towards her. A youngish girl with fair hair, wearing colourful overalls.

She noticed Ana's forlorn body language. "Everything all right?"

"I suppose so. I just learned why native species find it hard to grow round here."

The girl sat down. She had straggly blonde hair and Ana could see she wore a simple shirt and dark blue skirt under her overalls — almost as if she was still in school uniform. She was probably older than she looked. "Basically the ground is poisoned and will be for millennia when those skyscrapers fall down. There are three trillion tons of concrete and asphalt out there. We are in the 'stopgap' so to speak. We are racing against time to select and grow survival crops. We are finding ways to survive until enough land is recovered out there." And she waved in a roughly westerly direction.

"You think they will find a way to hold back the desert?"

The girl looked intense. "In theory it can be done. In ideal conditions, like no big hurricanes or floods or fires to destroy the work."

"In theory," mused Ana.

"Yes, in theory."

It was devastating. All these people. Hanging, on the edge. Ana felt a sudden rush of compassion. "And do they all know?"

"They know. Let's walk over to the rose garden. We kept the rose garden. Beauty is very important. It smells wonderful right now."

Ana was crying, silently, inside. She had been stupid and naïve to think New York was the foundation of a brilliant and sustainable way of living. Well maybe it was, but it was the fragility of it all which affected her. Yes, fantastic things were happening here, maybe the world could recover. But now she was in a form of shock. Jake worked out there, in the desert, with the silent hopes of millions resting on his shoulders. The enormous fragility of the undertaking was only now sinking in. One bad storm, just one, could lead to an irrecoverable state of starvation for everyone in this city and beyond. The larger part of humanity, not just here, but everywhere was just one big storm from extinction. It had been a theoretical situation to ponder this on the lush green slopes of Llanthony valley. Here in the big city she knew the people, they had smiles and love and a sense of peace around them, and they knew. They all knew.

An hour later Jake walked the horses up to the steps of the rose garden. He took one look at her blotched face and her blank eyes and understood. Sooner or later everyone had that look. It was the final bereavement for which there was no consolation.

She had been sitting here, alone, for some time and it was getting dark and she had not noticed the increasing coldness in the air. He took the blankets off the horses and spread them on the ground.

"Come," he said, as he lay her on the ground. "I see your penny has dropped. We'll stay here till sunrise." And he unfolded a small pouch of hazelnuts and blueberries. "I won't let you starve, at least not tonight."

They smiled, weakly.

Chapter 7
The Wolf

"So how many children are there in the city?"

Ana was back on the rooftops planting in a new experimental crop of groundnuts. Containing three times the protein of a potato, but with the disadvantage of needing three years to pass before harvesting, they were going to be a long shot. It was a risky decision, but the most favourable soil composition had been concocted — using copious amounts of composted chicken manure which was now in a positive supply — and the bag system could be said to be ideal for them.

"Are we counting? We're not counting. It is an individual decision, well, in theory. We're not making a thing about it either way." It was Lydia, deadly serious. "Can we feed the mouths we've got? We can't feed the mouths we've got. People keep coming here. More coming than leaving, I guess. If they make it. Children don't happen anyway. How do I know?" And she shrugged nonchalantly. "Plastics, radiation, vaccines... could be anything. I expect someone is working on it, but it's the kind of priority you need like a hole in the head."

Ana had only seen three children — the ones playing with boats in the street streams. Three children in the entire city.

Around them many people were quietly and quicky getting on with the work. The always unreliable weather forecast was predicted to be heavy rain, so they worked faster and more quietly than usual. The usual banter was missing. The mood was more than quiet, or maybe less. It was not the tranquillity of other days, it was oppressive, sombre. The rain could mean many things — high winds, storms. Tornadoes could whip themselves out of nothing, rain could mean hail. Hail could mean the ruination of crops. Calm sunny days were a false security. Everything that wasn't downright unpleasant was a false security.

Ana and Idris had arrived in a period of relative calm, but they had not understood that. Everyone was in good spirits as they are the world over when the sun shines and the breeze flutters and there is enough food and drink to go round.

Lydia stood up and stretched her aching back.

"Maybe you should take a break," suggested Ana.

Lydia looked up. From their high vantage point she could see clouds forming to the south-west. Innocent white bundles of fluff with only a hint of disguised grey menace.

She sank back to her knees, the padded cushion absorbing the brunt of the manoeuvre. "I'll do some different work tomorrow, but right now we have to plant this roof in double time and decide whether or not to cover it." This time there was no disguising the fearful look she gave the sky.

Already signs of increased activity in the people around signalled haste and urgency. Suddenly it was decided not to finish the planting, but to take the potted young groundnut bushes into the sheltered top floor of the building they stood on.

Patchwork sheets of canvas were hauled across the planted beds and laid out like furled sails. The work was switching from planting to protection. Slats were being driven hard down onto the frames of vegetable beds to shield them from wind and rain. Metal anchors were being pulled out of the roof surface for hooking the corners of protective sheeting down.

Ana looked to the south-west. Nothing much seemed to have changed. Did everyone know something she didn't know? This sudden rush of energy bordered on panic.

"Grab this," said a young man who was hauling out the folds of a what looked and felt like a giant sail. "Hold on tight whilst I pull it."

She understood. She angled her entire body weight into hanging onto that corner, whilst several other people pulled and tugged the vast sheet from various angles until it was almost smooth. They worked with speed, fastened it down to the anchors, then they were gone.

"Good job!" said Lydia. "That has to be an all-time record. Only another hundred rooftops to go."

"What if it doesn't rain?"

"Then they will have done a fire drill. Let's go down. It'll be dangerous up here if the wind starts."

Ana had to assume everyone knew something she didn't know, for at street level something similar was happening. Every pair of hands was anchoring something, dragging something indoors, covering something. She didn't need to be asked. Everything movable had to be taken inside the nearest doorway. No chances taken.

In a matter of two hours an early, dark night consumed the city. Few lights burned. Ana went in search of Idris and found him in cheerful conversation with some folk of his own age. He was fed and happy.

She walked the few blocks to where Jake was staying. Lightening flashed, then the rumble of distant thunder. The sound of a brooding monster echoing through the deserted streets.

Jake was not in the common rooms. She went to his sleeping area. A small cabin of a room giving privacy but not much space. On the bed Jake sat, his head in his hands. He did not look up when she spoke. She knelt down in front of him and smoothed his hair back. It was wet. His shoulders shook, just slightly. She embraced the crying man gently.

"Tell me."

"A landslide. Huge. We lost a hillside. A vast hillside of skilfully planted abundance. Many young people are missing. We must have done something wrong. I need to find out. I need to think it through."

She cradled him onto the bed. Those big feet, those big hands, that long silky hair, she put her arms round it all. He was fragile. He was allowed to break, and she rocked him like a baby.

Someone brought food and drink, and closed the door so that they could have some privacy. This man. This large, strong, clever man, weeping on the inside, weeping on the outside, weeping for the hillside, for the missing, for the endless weeks of toil under a burning sun, for the plants and trees and the dreams of a verdant future.

And it wasn't over.

From deep inside the building could be felt the vibration of enormous thunderclaps. The single light in their room flickered crazily.

"I have to see, to know, to feel," said Jake, and he hauled his large frame off the bed.

"I'll come with you," said Ana.

She wasn't sure that he heard her, so she just followed him down the corridor onto the street. The heavy menace of rain started to reveal itself, and the wind gathered in gusty billows, belligerently working its way round the corners of buildings, shaking the trees.

The rain came, first in big warning plops the size of dinner spoons, then suddenly a deluge. Jake walked carelessly out into the storm, a man broken. His face wet, tortured, sobbing, turned to the sky and he howled the long mournful agony of an animal in distress. For mesmerising minutes he seemed to transform before her eyes and take the spiritual form of a wolf, wailing forlorn notes of desperation into the elements. Then he folded, crouched onto his haunches, head in hands.

After a while he looked up and saw Ana, standing long and thin, arms limply by her sides, her clothes soaked through and stuck to her skin, still, transfixed at the surreal scene she had just witnessed. For a while they stayed immobile, looking at each other, reaching out with their eyes through the curtain of salty rain, passion accelerating.

She felt herself weaken. She had seen the untamed animal. Desire, compassion, raw emotion emanating from his entire body and reaching hers in pulsing swells of carnal longing. The angry onslaught of driving rain and wind pushed at her, tearing at her hair and clothing.

He unfolded effortlessly and moved towards her. Intent clear on his face, the storm parting before him.

His hand reached to the back of her sodden hair and pulled her head back, roughly, and he bent his weeping face down to hers, and kissed her hard on the mouth. She stood limp, completely overcome by this aura of unbridled masculinity, his consuming passion, his physical determination. She couldn't help herself. The rain, the storm, the grief, the animal in him, they combined to unleash in her the most potent orgasm she had ever had — before he even touched her. She gasped loudly in surprise at her own reaction. He pulled her close and thrust his hand between her legs and she sobbed and cried out again and again in soaring ecstasy until she could take no more, then he gently carried her collapsing body back into the room, and lay her on the bed, taking off his clothes, and drawing her gently onto his erect penis, slowly, surely penetrating her deepest sensual pleasures, and rocking her to ever more merciless rapture until she was practically unconscious, and only then did he allow himself one final climatic, euphoric explosion of sexual glory.

Dawn. First light. Gloom. Ana and Jake Dakotah stuttered awake, feelings mixed, but spirits one. He knew what would be found outside. She did not. She only suspected.

There was no breakfast.

Gingerly they walked outside. Silence. No wind or rain, just people wordlessly picking up the bits and pieces littering the ground. Shaking their heads, stooped with sadness, inconsolably trying to console one another.

Trees were uprooted. The great protective sails ripped and crumpled, just tatters in the trees. A wild tornado had screamed through the city, tearing up everything in its path. Broken glass, broken buildings, broken everything. Broken people. A scene of mental and physical devastation.

"Has it been this bad before?" asked Jake of a man standing listlessly in the road.

The man looked at him. Then looked away, and sobbed, hiding his crumpled face in the crook of his elbow.

"Ana, I think someone should find out the scale of the damage. I'm going to run across town and gather information. You stay here and do what you can."

He set off in a wolf-like gait which he could keep up for hours. It was something between a jog and a lollop. Loose, unhurried, relaxed, vibrant health oozing from every pore. She watched him with pride and renewed desire as he turned the corner, then moved off in the opposite direction to find her son.

Damage reporting was not interested in real estate — as long as the buildings were not supporting edible crops, it wasn't even interested in people missing or injured. That was a matter for the hostels and medics. Damage reporting was about survival. Human survival. Individuals were of less concern than apples, or barley, or beans.

There were arguments in the street. Fear was leading to fright, and fright to fight. The shallow burial of anxiety sifted itself to the surface and the moment bordered on violence.

"I told you the city was not the best place to be," shouted one man to another.

"So tell me a better place," said his neighbour.

"We're going to starve here. I told you we would."

"We were already starving, that's why we came in the first place."

A small crowd was gathering. Unhappy, confused, undirected. Powerlessness giving rise to angry feelings. The mood became increasingly volatile.

Ana and Idris hung together, wondering how all this was going to be managed. It appeared it was not being managed by anyone at the moment. People on the periphery were standing round looking helpless. No one stepped forward to organise. Anarchy in terms of non-hierarchical self-organising groups was letting itself down. Ana had a moment of inspiration. She might be the newcomer, but she wasn't about to witness any form of societal breakdown if she could be of help.

Positive activity was needed.

"Come and help me check out the roof gardens," she shouted to the groups standing off against each other. "We need to make an inventory of everything as quickly as we can. If everyone helps we can get it done in a day."

"Why? It's all hopeless," came the retort.

"It's only hopeless if we don't all get a move on. You'll need to find others and bring them into the plan. Please hurry. Food will go to waste if we can't sort this out today."

The situation diffused. She suggested they self-organise into different teams and do two blocks between them. The idea seemed to have the desired result.

Quickly they devised the main headings to report on — percentage of compost useable, percentage of plants retrievable, percentage intact, how long it would take to replant, number of people required and so on. It was the only way to get through this disaster. Positive action, fast.

The power was down, so it was hard work going up staircases, even on the low rise, which Ana and Idris decided to visit initially.

The first roof was at least half destroyed, but sixty to seventy per cent retrievable. They made notes of the type of plants, state of compost bags, beehives, shielding devices such as fences, covers, chicken coops. Any structural damage to the building, access et cetera. Ana and Idris were a good team. She dictated, he made notes, and together they formed conclusions. By lunchtime they had done five buildings and set up a contact point.

Ana suggested contact points be available every two blocks or so. Already people were bringing reports of damage. Ana started to compile them. Lists were constructed, calculations made. How much of the harvest was left, how much could be saved, how many people would it sustain and for how long. It was necessary, but haphazard.

The data was pulled together and teams quickly despatched to make horticultural repairs, to save what they could of the food supply. Structural repairs could wait. Nobody minded that some buildings might be unsafe. The mission was clear. Decisions were made on the hoof by the people most qualified to carry them out.

Clarity in the face of disaster was universally appreciated, and Ana began to understand her strengths. She could calculate quickly. She could organise. Everyone knew what to do, but they had been unsure whether or how to do it.

She asked for weather forecasts, the approximate trajectory the twister had taken, how many people were in the immediate vicinity, how long it would take to get the power up and running, and who was making the next meal for them all. She worried about water contamination and sent someone to check on the sea level and associated damage. Idris stood in awe. His mother had grasped the flailing reins of despondency and turned them into a flurry of organised activity. He was rather proud of her.

Jake returned at the end of the day, glistening beads of sweat from the many miles of running. He had probably loped through a couple of marathons. He put his hands lightly on her shoulders as she bent over some notes at a trestle table, concentrating hard. She looked up. To her he was a beautiful sight. The darkness of skin, the profile of Crazy Horse and the mane of a lion. What a distraction. She tore herself away from desirous thoughts. She wanted to ask him what he had found, but something in his look held her back.

She didn't need to know everything.

Chapter 8
The Cost

The next day found Ana surrounded by people eager and willing to work, but again largely without direction. She once again assumed the responsibility for organising. Years of home-grown survival through the snowy winters and blistering droughts of Wales certainly helped.

"Gather everything remotely edible. Leaves, flowers, fruit, roots, twigs and stalks. We need everything. Wash in cleaned water only. No rainwater, no grey water. The last thing we need is illness."

The plan was to make soups of the scraps, to bottle the undamaged, to hastily replant what was saveable. Teams went straight to work. Glad for the opportunity not to mourn.

A young woman standing beside her suggested someone go and investigate the underground horticultural system and report on the state of it. She grabbed a piece of paper and pen and quickly disappeared in the direction of the nearest subway. Ana sent Idris down after her with a solar torch. It could be dangerous down there if the light had failed. He ran swiftly after her, searching in the gurgling waters of the subway, calling out. Others joined him. She was never seen again. So many were lost that day.

It transpired that their part of the city had got off lightly. The area around East Twenty-Third was on the fringes of the main path of the tornado. Other areas had lost everything. No one said it out loud, but it seemed that thirty per cent of the city's food supply was irretrievable or just plain gone. Subject closed. Subjects open were about how to make the best of what remained.

Instructions of what to do filtered out through the city as if by osmosis. Best practice was quickly picked up and efforts quickly made to feed half a million people on the scraps of the city's storm damage. Ana preferred not to think about the numbers for now, just the possible.

The sun broke through the receding layers of storm. Solar cookers were dragged out. Old ones, new ones, home-made ones, big ones, small ones. Rows of people sat on the sidewalks, sifting and preparing the scraps of edible matter for washing and cooking. Cooking on solar is slower than most other kinds, so the main meal would not be ready much before evening. The bakers, the most valuable stalwarts civilization had ever provided, were well in advance of everyone else, and fresh bread was already appearing on the street. The smell was deliciously heartening. The few blocks around East Twenty-Third were going to be all right for a while, but the future was anyone's guess.

More damage reports filtered through. It was fine enough to talk about the disaster when you were eating freshly baked bread.

"We'll leave soon," whispered Ana to Idris as they stood stirring vast pots of leaves. "Tomorrow I'll investigate the situation with the boat, if it's still in one piece."

Idris looked at her bleakly. "Surely we should stay and help."

"We are two more mouths to feed, and maybe the best time to take to the sea is just after a disaster like this. It's not sustainable Iddy. This place, this city. I admire the spirit and the enterprising nature of these people, and I'm impressed with the overall mechanics, but survival here will be marginal at best, especially if there is little-to-nothing coming in from the hinterland."

The subway system had been flooded with salt water. Not all of it, but a significant amount. Lower Manhattan had been almost entirely subsumed by the sea. The Brooklyn Bridge, already damaged, no longer crossed the East River. Long Island was slowly being cut off, as was Manhattan. The power grid was down with little hope of it coming back again. Humanity had polluted itself back to the Stone Age.

Jake came back from his second foray into the areas of most damage. There was an increasingly bleak look about him. His shoulders hung a little lower than they had the day before. Ana looked up, compassion in her heart, and braced her mind for bad news.

"Remember the Botanical Gardens in the Bronx? The place where we stayed in the rose garden... there is no good way to say this…" His voice tailed off and his eyes became distant. He turned away so that she could not see his face. "Gone. Smashed to bits. All of it. Wrecked. Many died trying to save the plants and the libraries."

The man hadn't recovered from the devastating landslide which had buried so many of his Generation Restoration, the young people he was so proud of, working against all the odds to force back the deserts. More than likely, that weather event was the turgid root of the same storm which cut its relentless swathe across Manhattan Island.

"The library, that treasure of knowledge, is almost completely gutted. It was such a strong building, it could withstand the tornado, but fire from the inside… it's a disaster. Terrible, terrible loss to the future generations. I tried to salvage a few things. We have put the remnants of the books in what we hope is a safer place. But there is no such thing as a safer place anymore. We thought they would be safest where they were. We were crushingly wrong."

Ana remembered the happy day they had ridden together on horseback to the beautiful gleaming wedding cake structure of the glass houses. They had looked pink in the rosy sunlight, and in her remembered mind they were indeed pink. Frothy layers of perfectly proportioned tiers, missing only the statues of a bride and groom to top it all. She remembered also that it was the day her 'penny dropped'. The day reality triumphed over hope.

She put her arm across his shoulders. "Maybe you are here to help meet these problems. Maybe it is your calling."

He turned and put a hand on her shoulder, looking her straight in the eye. "Maybe it is yours."

Chapter 9
Shifting Paradigms

Jake Dakotah was crouched down on his haunches across the road from where Ana was working, contemplating the wonder she had become, and loving her all the more for it. She did not see him there. She was busy as usual organising, planning, sitting cross legged in her long patchwork skirt, her skirt of generations, deep in thought. Her mind was full of ideas, but one by one she discounted them. For example, she had thought of dividing the city into manageable parcels, to enable tighter organisation, then history reminded her that colonialism was always intent on dividing up areas, land, mountains, even the oceans, and she was sure settler-colonialism had contributed to the mess they were in now. Arbitrary lines across continents had prevented the sharing of resources, the movement of people, and often animals too. Conflict, starvation, war and death had been the result. The new deserts were strewn with carcasses of land animals who would once have migrated with the seasons. Visions of emaciated people frantically clawing at steel and concrete border fences, desperate for water, or food, or both. The scenes had not been played out on media screens for fear that humanity might be moved to act in a humane way, to tear the borders down from the other side and let them in. Millions of animals died. Who knows how many people. No, it was all kept quiet. No one with a shred of humanity could get anywhere near a border in the early days.

Extraction economies, slavers, greed and power, consuming all available resources without replacing or even acknowledging the debt to nature. Ana felt she was in the vanguard of a change of paradigm. As Einstein so simply put it, 'The level of thinking which created a problem (or set of problems) will, by definition, be unable to solve this problem.' A new level of thinking was required.

She wanted to rise above the mistakes of the past. History — if you could read between the lines — had mapped out all the follies of humanity. Written as it may have been by the victor, the omissions were clear enough. You just had to look for them. Wisdom and learning would help to discover better ways. For now, a loose social anarchy, the combined power of a busy community and fair leadership, would make sure that whatever resources they had, were available to all.

She had run away from London when disaster struck, and her first instinct was to run from New York. It was cowardly, but the anguish in both these places had felt too much for her to bear. However, fate had intervened, and her exit route from New York had been removed — for a few months at least — and she was forced by circumstance to face her demons. It turned out that her demons were more or less the same as everyone else's, but years of motherhood and survival, her old Welsh teacher, and something until then unknown inside her, grit maybe, had forced an internal reckoning, and her heart had responded and risen to the challenges, even as her mind was confused as to how she did this.

Ana had, eventually, organised the whole city — or maybe the whole city had encouraged her to organise it. Many had left, thousands heading in long bedraggled lines to the far north-east where trees still stood and rain still fell. The quickly becoming overcrowded north-east, because there was nowhere else to go, nowhere else left. The west was pure desert, the plains were desert, the mid-west a parched and hellish landscape. All shrivelled to death under a baking atmospheric heat dome which seemed never to move. Fires marched across the country creating their own electric storms, which in turn created more fires and so on. If the heat and humidity didn't kill you, the fires would. Money and technology did not march in to save the day as had been so glibly promised. The fantasy of business as usual finally demoted itself to a distant dream.

The city dwellers, desperate, marginalised, turned away from violence and selfishness, put their faith in each other, and had not questioned Ana as she moved from area to area, explaining what would work best, examining their resources, making decisions. It was not authority she felt, or power, or position. She simply felt able.

By her side, always, was Idris, Jake and Red. They were sometimes joined by the ever-buoyant Aoko when her health permitted. They were a team of sorts, and like everyone else they were permanently hungry. Visible weight loss was becoming almost a badge of honour, for long-term survival was more important than short-term gratification.

In short discussions, every resource was weighed up and a plan for the corresponding couple of blocks drawn up. To Ana it was simplicity itself, but painstaking, and impossible without hyper-local knowledge. Storage, priorities, safety, numbers of mouths to feed, numbers of mouths which could be fed, nutritional values, stocks of grain, potential harvest — all these together made the formulation for living, keeping going, just a bit longer, feeding the hope. Humanity had been dragged back to a cosmic beginning with no time for evolution. More of the young and the strong went out to the hinterland to reclaim some sort of future, the rest worked on innovation and survival.

Somewhere out there, there might still be a government, making useless laws and taking useless votes, it was a standing joke. Maybe the government just dissolved in a soup of its own uselessness, nobody really knew. Government in the archaic sense of the word had ceased to be relevant in the tree-planting years, when the people knew in their hearts what had to happen and had given up waiting for legislation. One of the most beautiful outcomes of not having a vested-interest government was the absence of intolerance and the death knoll of racism. Everyone was equally on the brink of disaster, and there was, finally, enough love to go round.

Jake looked at her, at the blossoming of a fully formed human, projecting a compassion which sees the inherent worth in all living things. He had fallen deeply in love with her the moment he first saw her, and the subsequent weeks had only deepened that feeling. It was like a calling, to be beside her. Just to be near her was a pleasure deeper even than the sight of a flourishing hillside of newly planted trees. He knew she would leave one day. He understood why.

Ana had asked Jake to come with them. His experience in greening the desert would be invaluable in the Middle East, but Jake had never been on a boat, let alone crossed an ocean. His country sang loudly to him with the ancient songs of his ancestors. His land was all but returned. Devastated and broken though it was, it needed him, and those like him. He looked upon this great social and agrarian change not as a disaster, but as a gift, and Ana knew it would be like tearing himself into two if he was to leave. She did not want to be parted from him, but did not push. Her understanding was as deep as her love.

When the opportunity to catch a ride on a transatlantic yacht eventually presented itself, Jake and Ana lived out their personal tragedy in silent torment. Apart from the weeks Jake had been in the desert with Idris, teaching him the rudiments of landscaping for rain and fertility, Jake and Ana had spent almost every sleeping and waking moment alongside each other, savouring the smell, the aura, the tangible strands of magic which drew them close even though they might be apart.

The boat which had carried Idris and Ana westwards across the Atlantic, had escaped in a hurry before the great tornado hit. Few boats hung around long anyway. There was always a storm of some sort, and when your moorings are half-submerged bicycle racks there is too much risk of underwater damage. Ana let it be known that she was looking for a ride back, and there came a chance of hitching a ride on a small vessel in November, sometime after what used to be known as the hurricane season, which sometimes still was the hurricane season, and she was making plans accordingly.

Confident that the bulk of the city dwellers would scrape through the winter if nothing calamitous was to strike, she knew she should take this last chance to see Hania. The shrapnel travelling through his brain would eventually kill him, and it was paramount in her mind that he meet his son.

A few days before they left, the three of them sat and broke bread at the water's edge, now calm, in the uncanny no man's land just below First Avenue and East Twenty-Third. The FDR Drive loomed lazily out of the water like the senseless memorial to the fossil fuel industry it was. Small dinghies nudged against it, and the ramparts were strewn with fishing rods eager to catch today's supper.

The East River was blue and clean, full of fish. Not far away rose the misty fountain of whale spouts. The wind had changed, taking the atmospheric pollution from the burning deserts of Ohio and Kentucky away from the east coast. The view was benign and clear.

"Northern rights," exclaimed Idris, pointing in excitement.

"Humpbacks," countered Jake, who knew so much about the land, yet so little about the sea.

It was another of those glorious days when you could almost forget about climate change — once you got used to skyscraper islands. If you looked past the broken windows and tattered balconies they almost looked picturesque.

A whale breached. The sight forever spectacular.

"Northern right!" said Idris and Jake together, delighted to see a species once thought to be functionally extinct, their demise mainly due to entanglement in the fishing gear of factory fleets which were given free rein to plunder the oceans, in the dreadful past, before.

"All we had to do was stop killing them," said Idris. "Too simple."

They sat in wonder, as several whales propelled themselves blissfully into the air, fins outstretched, and crashed back to the surface in gigantic waves of foaming water. Nature was somehow finding its way through a century of pollution and plastic, and there would be human survivors, somewhere, when all the fires died down, and the storms weakened. Maybe a hundred years from now, maybe a thousand. Half of all species on the planet had been lost, but there was still the joy of the other half. There was room for hope. Babies would be born. A new, possibly nomadic, way of life would tide humanity across the abyss.

"You were here for a reason," mused Jake. "Both of you. This city avoided panic because of you, Ana. You guided them away from destructive behaviour and helped them progress. I know they do not want you to go."

Idris got up and moved away to give them space for a last intimate discussion. Embarrassed, slightly.

Jake Dakotah, earnestness in his eyes, turned to Ana, and slowly, carefully opened his heart to her. "Our people believe that all of creation is sacred and that all people share one heart though they are many. This I know, your heart and mine are one. I do not want you to go."

He had not articulated the words before this moment. Gruffly spoken and few, words were not his favourite medium.

Ana lifted his brown muscled arm and wrapped it around her neck.

"My love, my joy. It is you who must stay. Your real nature and your real gifts are about making that desert green — greener even than it was before. Jake Dakotah, the force of your life is out there. It is your battle, your longing, and stopping the advancing desert will be your greatest accomplishment.

"I can only offer you human love. But you carry on your shoulders the love and hopes of a million forsaken ancestors. It is you who will take back the land — not from the white settlers who stole it and destroyed it, for they have already gone, but from the force of nature which holds it in terrifying balance, holds it ready for those who have the guts and fortitude to reclaim it. You cannot do it alone, and that's the point, but no one out there can do it without you. Your strength, your compassion, your wisdom. Of course you can't come with me any more than I can stay. We both know what we have to do. A great paradigm shift is happening now, we are on the cusp, and it's fragile, and it needs our guidance, wherever we are."

They stared out beyond the river to the floods of Greenpoint and beyond. Each imagining the long voyage across the Atlantic to the Straights of Gibraltar, and from Gibraltar to the Mediterranean and Gaza. It was almost an uninterrupted straight line of travel.

They drew closer, a more uncertain future could not be imagined.

"Alive or dead I will come back."

He pierced her heart with a look of ferocious intensity. "And I will find you."

Chapter 10
Constant Vigilance

She was a forty-foot, fixed keel sailing yacht of dubious origin and even more dubious seaworthiness.

When Ana and Idris stepped aboard, they hesitated. The skipper was all gung-ho and fighting talk and exhibited the complete inability to pronounce an 'h' in any word except where it wasn't wanted. He extolled the virtues of his craft, his 'magical hadditions' as he called them. The solar cells, the water turbines, the reverse osmosis desalinator with 'remarkable' filtration. "Remarkable!" he insisted. "Remarkable!" in a vocal range which went from the gravelly depths of East London to something approaching shrill adolescent jubilation.

"Two berths fore and two berths haft. Plenty of room mi 'earties!" And he rubbed his hands and laughed with glee because there really was anything but plenty of room amongst the boxes and ropes, and assorted gear stashed about the place.

"Usual payment," he muttered in a growling Cockney accent, and looked Ana up and down with a slight wink and what she took to be a lascivious glint in his eye. "You can call me Ishmael! Haw Haw!" And he laughed again at his own hilarity, which was not a joke considering the voyage they were undertaking — at least not a joke to Ana who had more than a passing acquaintance with a book called *Moby Dick*. It didn't cross her mind for some while that she hadn't understood exactly what he meant by this.

'The usual payment', didn't mean that she should do the cooking. She had nothing to trade but her skin, and sex was becoming a viable means of exchange where money didn't buy you anything. It was a means to an end.

Idris knew. It had been the same coming over, and he just kept a low profile. Ana had explained before that she really didn't mind. The men she had traded with had been decent enough, what's more they sometimes were happy enough with the promise of sex, or maybe just a bit of foreplay. There was no way she felt compromised, and although someone like Jake Dakotah might prefer it otherwise, he would also know from his own tribal roots that monogamy was hardly a rule.

Jake left the city first, in a convoy of patched-up buses crammed full of the young and strong, eager to join Generation Restoration. There could only be one outcome to this project, and they had to make it happen at all costs. Boys, girls, old, young. Age was no barrier. Health and strength the requirements.

Ana and Jake said their tender goodbyes in the pre-dawn light of a late December morning. They held each other tight, as if to squeeze out darkness and depression from between them, and all around shimmered a clear, early light, and the sun rose hopefully.

The old electric buses whirred slowly up the all-too-aptly named old Indian trail of the Weckquaesgeek — the end of the wet meadow — or Broadway, as the Europeans called it. The convoy would press on to the new frontier, somewhere in Pennsylvania, where life met death, and desert and green locked horns in a fight to the death.

There being no other suitable boat in sight, Ana and Idris packed their few belongings and walked the short way to the water, now a little nearer than it had been a few months ago, somewhere around what used to be called Battery Park.

On their arrival at the impromptu mooring they were greeted, to their sincere shock, with the sound of a brass band playing all manner of joyful tunes — and a crowd! 'A Life On The Ocean Waves' was followed by a stirring rendition of 'The Liberty Bell', and a good many other heartening tunes. Many people had taken a couple of hours off their projects, woken early, and come to the water's edge to see them off. They were cheering their thank yous, banging drums and showing appreciation in whatever noisy way came to mind. One woman brusquely stepped forwards and planted a huge diamond and sapphire brooch in Ana's hand. It was Lydia.

"Ain't no use to me honey," she laughed. "Ain't no use to no one much, but maybe it'll help you in some way. Who knows, you might get lucky. Who knows, we might all get lucky!" She chuckled, and kissed Ana fondly.

"*Mazel tov*." And she closed Ana's fingers over the shimmering stones.

Red was there, and Aoko, and almost everyone they had ever met. It was crazy. Ana and Idris jumped onto the boat, waving furiously. "Please leave quicky," implored Ana as she disappeared below deck, embarrassed.

The skipper cast off with expert ease. The *Constant Vigilance* trembled slightly as she headed out into the river breeze. Ana and Idris went back on deck for a last wave goodbye, and the boat slipped gently onto the sparkling Hudson, past the green-weathered profile of Liberty, still standing, still brandishing her lamp, with the passive face of Bartholdi's mother still staring south-east to the fires of Philadelphia even as the sea rose and lapped at her pedestal.

They faced into the stiff breeze, Ishmael grunting a bit as he laboured with the sails, and the fourth member of the crew appeared on the deck.

She gracefully extended a lean brown arm, little silver bangles tinkled to her wrist. Her waving grey hair, loose and long, spread across her face as the gentle wind grew stronger. Her eyes crinkled kindly. "I am Minas." She seemed to flutter with the breeze, her hareem trousers skimming slender thighs, and hanging in brightly painted folds to her ankles to reveal long slim feet. Perfectly formed feet.

Ana caught her gaze and could not look away. There was something intriguing in this older woman, something mesmerising and desirous.

The day being reasonably calm, they sat out on deck and ran through the drill. Ishmael (was that really his name?) gruffly informed his passengers that he had sailed the *Constant Vigilance* single-handed across the Atlantic a few times and a few times more. He needed a cook, a cleaner, a rota for lookout, and complete obedience. There would be rotating four-hour shifts, and he would take a six-hour shift at night — ten p.m. until four p.m. The rest was up to them. He then took them round the boat on a general inspection tour, pointing out some basic equipment such as first aid, life jackets and barometer. Apparently there was sketchy radio contact with one or two of the remaining functional weather satellites, but it was just as good, if not better, to look at the thermometer, the air pressure, and make up your own mind about the wind direction. If they met another craft they might heave-to for a chinwag. If the weather was not good, they might have to change course. No promises as to how long the voyage would take, where they would stop, how many detours, or indeed where they would eventually end up.

"You got it mateys?" he gruffed, with a hint of menace as if he would throw any suspected insurrectionists overboard if they did not immediately agree.

Idris liked it. The idea of an open-ended un-business-like adventure upon the high seas was appealing. Ana was less convinced, and Minas — who knew? Minas was almost silent on every matter, yet at the same time supportive and helpful. It was as if she could read their minds, and oddly as though they could read hers. On such a small craft it was alternatively welcome that she was not noisy, yet tantalisingly annoying that she volunteered very little about herself.

The first few days were smooth and balmy. They fished, they took turns on lookout, they kept the place ship-shape. Ana lovingly sewed some more pieces into her patchwork skirt. They were little gifts from those she had grown close to in the city. Chief among them was a piece of shirt belonging to the wild and passionate man she so reluctantly left behind. She smoothed the material gently with her warm hands until the creases were gone, and as she did so the memory of his hand against her skin renewed in her mind, and she wished for that sensual touch again. Skirt or not, he would always be with her, part of the shape she was becoming, part of the woman who would one day step out of this cocoon of a skirt and into her own full glory.

Remnants of material, remnants of her life. Her memories. Her past, her griefs, her joys. A large section of the garment was made of pieces from her grandmother's floral dress. It was of printed red and purple roses on a black satin background, the dress her gran was wearing in an old photo Ana had seen. There were scraps from her mother's clothes, from clothes Idris had worn as a baby, a toddler and almost all points in between. Her favourite was a little square of pale blue ducks from a sweater the toddler Idris refused to give up until he could no longer get it over his head. There were leftovers from dresses she had made, curtains, and a piece she had cut from the bandana the old Welshman had worn until he died. You could still make out the words of the Italian resistance song 'Bella Ciao' embroidered upon it. This was indeed a skirt of generations, but it was slowly rotting.

Minas sat in her habitual place close to the bow of the ship. Around her slim body was gathered a blanket of homespun wild sheep's wool, rough and slubby. She was gazing ahead, the wind taking her hair in ropes of thick grey, throwing it back away from her finely contoured face, and she stared passively ahead.

Idris was reading. He had got excited about the work being done in the American desert, and Jake Dakotah had given him, as a parting gift, one of the textbooks rescued from the ruins of the Botanical Gardens. It was about mycelium, the fungus-like colony of bacteria which spread across the land interacting with plants and soil to maintain health and weave it into fertile structures. He had it in his mind to create mats of mycelium as a forerunner to planting crops, and by his side was a dog-eared notebook full of ideas and experiments he wanted to try out when he got to Levanta.

Ishmael was studying the ship's barometer. The air pressure was dropping rather too quickly for his liking. Set in an old ring of polished brass, its spiny needle never lied. He suddenly changed the course of the boat, and they headed north.

"Ah, 'urricanes come further north every year. Feels like there's one brewing right now. Best get out of its way." He charged about the boat swinging the rudder and adjusting the sails. As he worked he winked his apparently lascivious wink, but looks can be deceiving. Ishmael had only one eye.

"Come down to the cabin later will you Ana." He called as he made good his work.

By the time Ana had finished her watch it was dark and spitting ice. They were not very far north, probably just a couple of hundred miles off Newfoundland, and there was practically no chance of finding an iceberg since the Blue Ocean Event of 2025, when the Arctic finally gave up the struggle to keep hold of its covering of icy white, and the resultant climactic tipping point tipped right over itself. The disappearance of the albedo effect of white ice reflecting heat back into the atmosphere gave space to the darker ocean, and absorption of heat accelerated. Some drifting islands of ice did remain, and although they were reportedly quite small, so was *Constant Vigilance*. It was best to do as her name suggested. Minas came up to take over the evening shift and Ana went down to make her first visit into the captain's cabin. It would at least be warmer than the deck.

"Aha!" exclaimed the skipper in his usual overabundant way. "Come and make yourself comfortable in my floating palace." And he waved his arm, insomuch as an actual wave was possible in the cramped berth, and beckoned her sit on the bed.

It was, to Ana's surprise, rather beautifully furnished with Turkish cushions and a coverlet of mirrored Indian tapestry. The wooden walls were polished oak, as everywhere on the boat, but they too were hung with exotic materials, and the overall impression was of a tiny Bedouin tent bobbing about in a desert of ocean.

She sat down. Ishmael winked, which was not a wink, simply a one-eyed blink, and got out a large pad of paper.

"I draw," he said, a new modesty in his rough-hewn voice. "I think I might be improving, but when there is only the wide blue 'orizon for company, it's 'ard to improve. Would you do me the 'onour of being my muse for the voyage?"

It was not what she expected.

She gathered about her this new information, and of course agreed. Obviously she was not sure of the exact nature of his drawing intentions, but considering her previous expectations, the outlook seemed favourable.

He asked her to undo the top buttons of her shirt, settled her down across the cushions, arranged her legs modestly and looked at her. The wink was disconcerting, but the real challenge was keeping still. Ishmael scratched away with charcoal on cartridge, and 'ummed' to himself now and then, deep in thought, then suddenly announced she should get some sleep and went up to join Minas on the deck.

Occasionally large seabirds kept them company, wheeling overhead, sometimes landing on the craft. Gulls, white-tailed eagles, even the great northern diver, resplendent in its checked tuxedo and striped bowtie. Sometimes the feathered friends stopped for a few hours or minutes, vaguely curious about these two-legged travellers, without fear, for whilst birds elsewhere might be hunted, up here on the roof of the world, their liberty was unbounded, and their populations grew in perfect harmony with the amount of fish available. Nature, always seeking balance, kept a tight check on things.

Thus the evenings in the northern waters passed, sometimes there was rain, sometimes wind, sometimes huge waves tossed them about for a few hours, just for fun. *Constant Vigilance* and her skipper kept a firm hand on whatever the weather could throw at them, and soon she was slipping around the roof of the world, effortlessly skimming the cheerful waters of a northern sea teeming with life. Huge shoals of fish. Big fish, little fish, flying fish, families of whales — of narwhal, beluga whale, blue whale, fin whale, humpback, minke, pilot whale, sperm whale — could all be spotted and identified as they sailed towards the Arctic Circle. Playful dolphins and pesky seals kept them close company, chattering excitedly as they raced the boat, always winning.

The southerly tip of Greenland came into view. Ishmael pointed to the huge metal stanchions pounded deep into the rock to support massive arrays of mirrors which covered almost the whole island continent. Even the vast inland Greenland lakes were covered in floating mirror arrays. It was a vision of desperation.

Binoculars and telescopes were passed around feverishly. The great reflecting mirrors had been built to try and hold back the warming. Most Greenland ice had been on land, and therefore the land melting had contributed disproportionately to sea level rise. Some said they caused a twenty-foot rise across the globe. All manner of high-tech fixes had been proposed, and tried, and found wanting. The Greenland mirrors had been the last joint world effort to tackle climate change head on. Thousands of enormous mirrors pointed to the sky, reflecting the heat of the sun back to the upper atmosphere. Underneath was a near permanent darkness, but little in the way of ice was forming. It was probably too late anyway. The Greenland ice melt had come after the major tipping points of desertification, glacier melt, and a global temperature increase of two degrees. The temperature was of course still climbing. Somebody, somewhere was monitoring the effect of the mirrors, but it was a long-term thing, and short-term details like survival got in the way. People of the future might wonder what they were for.

Ana was bouncing up and down in subdued excitement as she focused the powerful binoculars on the fragmented coastline of the vast island. There were a million birds or more perched on the crazy striped slopes of the nearest islands. Auks, puffins and kittiwakes. Birds she had never seen in her life before. Snow buntings, ringed plover, red-necked phalarope, owls and eagles… the list was extraordinary.

"Do you think they'll survive the warming?" she whispered to the world in general, a general awe having overtaken the inhabitants of the little boat.

"Plenty of food. Plenty of fish. Plenty of snow-free land. They've got a good chance as long as it doesn't get much warmer," said Ishmael in an unusually hushed voice. "There are inland birds too. Ducks and geese, eiders. Then the animals long ago imported by early settlers. Goats, reindeer, chickens and dogs. I haven't seen the big old polar bears for a while though, but fox, the 'airy musk ox, ermine, and Arctic wolf can all be seen if you know what you're looking for. I used to spend time 'ere."

"They'll have to keep the grazers enclosed though, so that trees and bushes can grow in future," said Idris, already planning the landscape of tomorrow.

Ana nodded. "Or maybe just leave it to develop as it wants. Not many humans to feed up here."

Idris languished back into thought. "True. Humans are always the problem."

The still cold waters clustering with tiny fragments of ice hung around the hull of their vessel.

"Best keep a sharp good lookout," said Ishmael quietly, scanning the waters. "We don't want any nasty surprises."

The outlying islands of Greenland looked raw and inhospitable. Ana traced the multicoloured strata of rock, worn smooth by a million years of glaciation and gasped at the magnificent barren landscape emerging from the sea. It was a wondrous sight. Alien, desolate, uninviting. These northern outcrops of ophiolite and zircon, four and a half billion years old, were safe from human invasion save a few small pockets of shelter. She felt like an intruder, as if their quiet glide past was somehow illegal, not wanted, a violation.

"Let's leave this in peace."

Ishmael smiled through his wiry beard. That is exactly what he intended to do. "Best to not even talk about it. Let it be."

They all nodded, and whispered agreement. In the church of pristine nature there was considerable respect.

"Look," whispered Idris in what could only be described as a stage whisper as he pointed to a slow-swimming giant, black and glossy, swimming amongst a group of humpbacks. Knobbly white patches of rough skin on its head were breaking through the water. Its fluke was broad and triangular, and it had no dorsal fin. "A right whale! We saw one around Manhattan, remember? Wow!"

Ishmael followed the gaze of Idris, tears began to run down his cheeks. "It's a young 'un!" he rasped. "They could be coming back! This is a bloody blessed day." He wiped his face, both seeing and unseeing eyes wept, and did not easily stop. The emotion in him ran silent and deep.

"You know I've been sailing this ocean for thirty years and it's been frighteningly empty for most of that time. Once, maybe three 'undred years ago, it teemed with some of the biggest mammals on earth. Blue whales and fin whales, sperm and 'umpback all gathered and fed in these rich and fertile waters.

"They were brutally 'unted back then, by men in rowboats and 'arpoons — the whalers. Each species in turn was slaughtered in this vile trade, until they were thought to be extinct. The whalers just moved on to persecute the next species. It took until the twentieth century to legally stop commercial whaling. By that time, me dears, it was almost too late. Most species were extinct as far as folk could tell. Maybe they'd killed all the males, or all the females. No one knew if they even could reproduce what with all the pollution and noise. But they 'ave! My God they 'ave!"

He scanned the waters again in awe, not even trying to wipe the tears away. "It's a wonder! A real wonder. A bloody, bloody miracle." And he wept openly as the majestic sight of humpbacks, rights and sperms glided by, softly churning the waters as they grazed the abundant krill and plankton together.

Ana wondered if this was the moment to bring up a subject which had been teasing her for some time. She tentatively ventured, with a sidelong look, "You know, I read *Moby Dick*, I understand what you are saying about the whalers and the extinctions, and I know what the first line of the book is."

Ishmael turned to her, a broad smile spreading across his face. "Few understand the true meaning matey. I wonder if you will."

"Well," she said. "I know it has biblical origins, and I know the mythology of Abraham's sons, Isaac and Ishmael, and the rivalries between them and their mothers. I always thought he got a raw deal. So why are you Ishmael. Did you choose it or is it your actual name?"

He dodged her question. "I worked on the reasoning for that first sentence for years, and eventually decided that the author used it because he wanted to convey, upfront, that his narrator was way less important than the story he was about to tell. I guess that's how I feel about myself."

"Wow. Interesting thinking." She cast her mind back to that vast volume of a book, and yes, the book was not about Ishmael at all. He was there all the time, but he did not divulge his personality, or if he did it was minimal. Yes, the bible myth has Ishmael as a lesser import than Isaac, so Melville might well have alluded to that. It was always an enigmatic beginning, the book, *Moby Dick*.

Ishmael — the non-biblical, non-literary variety — was pulling at his beard. "I am always less important than the people I carry. I am just the vehicle for the story. I take people to and fro, it is the people I carry who 'ave purpose."

"Yet," and Ana was thinking aloud at this stage, "Ishmael was the sole survivor of the ship, so maybe the reason for his survival was to tell the story, and the storyteller himself, in this case, was the vehicle for the story."

"So, if you must give me a name, call me Ishmael. I seek no other."

Ana smiled at him, warming to this odd one-eyed seafarer, satisfied with the conversation. The others had listened in, but were somewhat bemused.

"Call me Ishmael," said Idris, liking it. "I wonder if I will ever find a copy of that book."

Chapter 11
The Clone

They dropped south to warmer seas, the sun now setting on their right, and the hours fussed about with longer spells of daylight and balmy breezes. Not as warm as they used to be. The last gasps of the Gulf Stream struggled hopelessly against the freshwater melt of the Arctic, its temperate influence on the climate of Europe diminished. The prevailing westerlies were confused and no longer the dependable trade winds of yesterday. Nothing was as yesterday. Passage slowed.

"It's getting like the bloody Sargasso," Ishmael muttered under his breath, comparing the north-east Atlantic to the oft becalmed seas around Bermuda. "Gawd strewth. Even the weed is 'anging around 'ere."

He pointed out pale brown mats of bubble-like bladders poking just above the water. They were tangled with all manner of detritus. Some of it was piling up a foot high. Maybe more.

"And the plastic," said Idris dismally, eyeing half submerged bottles and containers clogging together with the seaweed. "Jeez," he said disgustedly, half under his breath. "What were they thinking of. This stuff isn't going to degrade for a thousand years. Why?" He looked around at no one in particular. "Why?"

They all knew why, and it made no sense at all.

"But look." said Ana, pointing the edge of a large mat of half rotted seaweed and plastic. "There is something living on it. What is it. A nest?"

Binoculars confirmed it was a nest and young chicks were cheeping excitedly in it. "Tern or gull?" suggested Ishmael, astonished. "Poor things think this is some kind of island."

"It is," said Ana. "Pretty much permanent too, with all the plastic involved."

"And there'll be small fish and crustaceans colonising it too I wouldn't wonder. Blow me down. I never thought I'd see the day." He shook his head in wonder. "It's come to this. And we'll eat the fish, and possibly the birds, and they'll have eaten the plastic. Ah well. We're all just 'anging on, so I don't s'pose it makes much difference either way."

One afternoon, when Minas was in her far-off mood with eyes fixed on a distant horizon somewhere beyond the actual horizon, Ana came and sat comfortably cross legged beside her.

"You look melancholy?"

Minas, torn reluctantly from her thoughts, cocked her head slightly and smiled in her quizzical way. "Not sad. Maybe forlorn, but maybe a little bit hopeful at the same time. I have a feeling of longing. Maybe for a place, or a home, or a person I never knew. A kind of homesickness for a country I may never have been to. Maybe it does not even exist."

Ana had never experienced such a feeling, in fact sometimes she experienced the opposite, an overarching excitement for the unknown which was to come. But she was adventurous and ready for the world, and the long journey was beginning to frustrate her. In any case, it was something of a breakthrough to be having such a definitively open conversation with this strange companion.

"Is it something from your past?" she asked, eager not so much to understand the context as to fathom the inner workings of this enigmatic woman.

Minas expanded her distant smile and spoke in the low timbre voice of enchantment. "I had an usual beginning, possibly unique. You see I'm a clone."

There was no immediately accessible response available. Ana felt inadequate. A clone was rarely heard of, rarely spoken about, taboo. There had been experiments, of course, but Ana had generally filed them in the 'too awful to contemplate' part of her brain. She had not known about long lived survivors. She was dumbstruck.

"My story is a strange one. Do you want to hear it?"

Ana nodded, already enthralled, slightly horrified.

Minas settled herself to face Ana. She was propped up on the roughly woven blanket as usual, and her voice spoke low and melodic. "There were fifteen of us, all alike, identical probably, growing up in an isolated clinic, with only each other for company. Almost no contact with the outside world, few books, and no preparation for what would happen when we were freed, as we eventually were.

"We were so scared, and were split up for our own safety. It was terrifying. You see we all looked and acted and spoke alike. We even had the same name. We were an experiment, both physically and psychologically. Oh my goodness we were so unprepared for a world of gods, and machines, and politics and disasters... but that was a long time ago.

"I eventually ended up in America, with a family who showed me nothing but kindness, but it was not possible for me to feel part of the culture, or any culture for that matter. We had been cut off for too long. My adopted family died in one of the pandemics. I do not yearn for the clinic, but my sisters, yes. We were together, isolated, for many, many years. We developed our own culture, our own language, our own view of the world outside. I think it is the memory of us, the thing which bound us, made us whole, possibly something in our genetic code which draws me back to my past self."

"Nostalgia?" ventured Ana, feeling somewhat inadequate for the conversation.

"No, that is too sentimental. It's beyond my heart, buried in my core. It feels as though we were collectively part of an organic whole, and separation broke something.

It feels like a place, but it is really a deep, deep longing for a connection or an emotion which existed, or could have existed, if we had lived a more natural life. The sea exacerbates the feeling, which is sadness, but maybe hope. The unreachable horizon, the calling of the starry sky, the wanting to belong, right back to distant universes of carbon atoms where all life began. It is a deep and unfathomable yearning."

"Maybe you are talking about hiraeth," said Ana. "It is a Welsh word. You pronounce it 'here-eyeth'. It does not translate, but I'm told it is all the things you have said and more. The old Welshman who looked after me when I gave birth to Idris taught me the word. He said hiraeth was a call to go to the place that would bring him as emotionally close as possible to where his spirit lives.

"I loved Wales and its people, their love of poetry and literature, their sense of place and magic. The old man said he would find his spiritual place wandering in the landscape, in nature, in the mountains, far from roads and villages and the clamouring trappings of human life. He would say the unsullied mountains of Wales made him feel close to his ancestors, and that is where he felt most at home."

"Here-eyeth," said Minas thoughtfully. "I think we were brought up near Wales, but we have no way of actually knowing for sure. Our clinic, before it was burned down, was remote and secure. We just picked up pebbles of information from cleaners and the like and did our best to categorise them and piece them together. Our view of the world outside had so many gaps." And she turned her gaze back out to sea in wistful sadness.

"What happened to the others?" asked Ana, uncomfortable about prying, but much too interested not to want more.

"Ah, that is the other great thing. I do not know. We did not stay in direct touch because of fear, which complicated the longing. We were taken to different places for our own safety. We were property, we were patents, we were owned by multinational pharmaceutical companies. I think some of us have survived. I feel it. I think I also feel it when we die."

Ana was intrigued and horrified, and unusually saddened by the whole concept of cloning. "Are you looking for your sisters now?"

"Yes, kind of, in a drifty way. We would easily know each other, I'm sure. We would 'feel' the presence of another. I will go back to find the place we came from. It seems fanciful, but there is the chance that now, in the turmoil of the world as it is, others will be thinking the same, and if our thoughts converge, maybe our solid matter will too."

Ana tried some encouraging words to cheer Minas out of her doldrums. "Maybe this is a good time. Maybe fewer people will be looking for you, and even if they found you, what would they do with you?"

Minas shrugged, and her silvery bracelets twinkled around her tiny wrist. "It has its risks, but what can we do? We are only whole when we are together. Apart, we are broken. We have lived apart as broken ones for too many years. Maybe we cannot be mended, but it is not just about us as a collective, I, we, have questions. I, we, would like to know what we were bred for, what the programme was, how they would have planned to use us if we had not escaped the clinic."

The words 'bred for' echoed around Ana's mind distastefully. Animals were bred. Humans were born. Maybe that was all wrong. Animals were born too. The word 'bred' had unpleasant connotations of slavery, experimentation, factory farming. Her thoughts conjured up any amount of unpleasant scenarios, from carriers of disease to limb replacements and all points in between. She said nothing.

Minas slowly returned her gaze to the horizon again. Her clear grey eyes did not see the air or the water or the shimmery place of uncertainty in between. They saw children, bronze-haired and grey-eyed, metal bed frames, people in white coats. It was a sadness she could not explain, this lack of love, connection, belonging.

"Next stop Ireland!" hailed Ishmael from across the boat, "If the winds are kind." And he laughed his crazy laugh, "Haw, Haw!" The irony being that there had been little in the way of wind for days.

Maybe the conditions which enabled the Sargasso, the slowly gyrating sea-within-a-sea, were being reproduced here in the north-east corner of the ocean now that the Gulf Stream was in its final act of dying. It was a grim thought for a man who had sailed the world's waters all his life. No sailor liked the Sargasso, and its morbid zombie child, the Bermuda Triangle. The once reliable ocean currents were in tatters, as were their faithful partners, the trade winds.

Minas turned her head and looked at the hair's breadth of land appearing on her horizon. "It feels nice. It smells nice. I've read about Ireland, I'd like to stop here a while. Maybe I can get to Wales from here." And she smiled that thin warm smile of hope infused with distant regret.

There was a definite need to replenish supplies, to run about, to escape the confines of the boat, and Ana and Idris thought it would be interesting to see how this part of Ireland was faring under changing conditions.

"Cool," said Idris. "Another new place to study." And he rolled out the charts with Ishmael.

"Do you think it's safe?" asked Ana. "They had a particularly lethal coronavirus here back in the twenties. The lockdown lasted years. Almost everyone over the age of twenty-five died. An immense tragedy."

"That was a long time ago Ana," said Idris. "They'll have herd immunity now."

"But we are from a different herd!" countered Ana. "The survivors would either have been genetically different enough to produce the right antibodies at the right time, or just highly resistant in the first place."

She heaved her shoulders up and down. New places always held a degree of uncertainty, exacerbated by the unknown, or the fear of it. The unknown unknowns, as someone with a crippled mind had once said.

"I know it was a long time ago. Maybe we can pull in to one of the smaller islands and check out the situation first. You know, the Precautionary Principle and all that." Ana directed this last thought towards Ishmael.

"OK. I can do precaution. We'll scout around a bit, but frankly most of these islands are godawful lumps of rock with cliffs punching through the sky and rocks to break diamonds."

He was right. The islands hanging around the west of Ireland were dark and craggy conglomerates stabbing mercilessly into the sky. Chamfered and cracked, angled and crushed, with gashes of pale onyx scarring their faces, these blackhearted cliffs were as foreboding as they were treacherous.

The *Constant Vigilance* kept her distance, creeping slowly round the boulder strewn promontories, all on board keeping a lookout for something resembling a beach or harbour.

A sudden current lurched at the boat, spinning her round, driving her towards a beachless cliff further out to sea. Ishmael uttered an exotic array of expletives and quickly turned the sail; Ana threw herself at the rudder.

Violent crashes of sea spray threw Minas from her perch at the bow, and she grasped at a rope to save herself being washed overboard. Idris, with the leap of a gazelle, bounded across the side of the boat and grabbed her arm. A gust came from nowhere, ballooned the sail, and took them sideways, careering desperately. The wind was almost gale force. It took them for miles, belligerently shunting the *Constant Vigilance* round perilous cliffs, poking boulders and dashing mountainous flumes of sea spray into their course.

It seemed inevitable that they would be wrecked on an unforgiving promontory looming directly in front of them. The shadow of the cliffs plunged them into darkness and the *Constant Vigilance* scraped recklessly round the maelstrom of water and rocks, the crew desperately trying to regain some form of control.

And then, suddenly, a beach.

Pale sands glistened.

"Strewth. That was too close for comfort," Ishmael muttered as he tightened the headsail for the cruise to calmer water.

Minas, unruffled, spread her hair to dry.

Heartbeats slowed. They giggled slightly as nervousness unwound itself from tense muscles.

The shallow bowl of the bay pulled them effortlessly to the inviting shore. Ana and Idris jumped out first, sea legs giving rise to grateful laughter as they wobbled unsteadily. The fine sand squished between their toes and tickled. Strangely warm was the water licking against their thighs as they waded to land. Between the shore and the land young trees grew, and beyond those the sloping shades of green rose gently, creating a dish-shaped shelter, facing to the south, picturesque and verdant. A small stream chattered, offering its fresh water to the saline bay.

Ishmael busied himself securing the boat. Minas stood on the bow, a slight breeze fanning dry the dampness in her baggy hareem pants.

From amongst the trees curious people came out to meet them, bronze of skin, lightly clad and barefoot. They were simply covered with roughly woven cloth, they carried poles and baskets. Cautiously the two groups of humans approached each other, slight suspicion, troubling concerns, bothersome thoughts. They both knew history even if history did not yet know them.

The visitors from the sea bowed to the people of the land, and the people of the land bowed back. One of them, looking up, saw Minas perched on her barky pedestal like a wispy monument floating in the breeze, and started walking towards her, hesitantly, quizzically, as if he recognised her. She looked mildly down as he approached.

The young man quickened his pace as he neared the boat, dropping his fish-pole. He walked into the water, his voice cracking with emotion, shouting, "Minas, Mama. Is it you? It is me. Artan!"

Minas listened, bemused, head tilted to one side as it always did when she was concentrating. It was her name. A rare enough name. But she had no son.

He stood below her, thigh deep in the water and extended his hand to her as if beseeching. She graciously extended her beautiful fingers, and the silvery bangles rippled down her arm, making their sparkling music.

Artan looked at the bangles and heard only the sound of painful remembrance. "It is you!" Tears came into his warm brown eyes. "I thought you were gone forever. I imagined you dead in that last great hurricane."

He pulled her gently down, catching her wispy frame in his arms, and she looked at him, into him, and he looked at her, into her slanted grey eyes, so familiar, and yet...

She pulled him into a gentle hug, and spoke very slowly, nodding, caressing the dark brown hair on the back of his head, pale eyes stinging. This, possibly her first link with her sisters, defied emotion. "I did not know we had a son, but I do know that you are surely him. Yes I am Minas. We are Minas, and I have a story to tell you, and you will understand that love indeed has no bounds."

They walked up the sandy beach of pebbles and shells and limestone crushed by the waves of a million or more years. Hand in hand. A son, confused, and a mother who wasn't a mother.

The two groups, having established such an extraordinary connection, began to exchange stories.

"Welcome to the Isle of Barwin!" announced a young woman surrounded by a gaggle of inquisitive children and chickens. "We called it after the girl who gave her life so that we could be here."

Artan smiled at the gabble of conversations erupting around him. Everyone wanted to know everything about everyone else in the shortest possible time. The island didn't get visitors. In fact, the last ones to arrive were Artan and his friends many seasons before, and they arrived by accident, much as the travellers in the *Constant Vigilance* had done.

"We have many stories. I expect you have many stories. Let us start to tell the tales tonight, when we have eaten, and the fire is still warm and we can savour every one."

They set up camp immediately as the days were short. A fire was lit just above the high-water line, and the small company toasted and shared their meal of fish and legumes as the stories were told in turn. The children always loved the story of Barwin the Barbarian, which no doubt had been embellished over the years. Of how Barwin survived with her grandmother in times of terrible hardship, of the Mallavirus which killed nearly everyone, of how the apple trees were cut down by violent gangs, how she stole food and buried it, how she met Artan, of the last great hurricane and the long journey which brought them to the island. They loved to hear how Barwin put her body between the cliffs and the boat and saved them all. They always went quiet when the part came where she died, but that even in death she joined them, a hero. The tale of Barwin was a tale for all time, for all thought, and the children would lay down to sleep thinking how they too would like to be heroes.

As the long dusk melted into a fine still night, Minas told Artan her story, her closeted upbringing with the fifteen cloned sisters, the rescue, and subsequent escape to scattered winds, they knew not where. She explained that they were all called Minas. It stood for Missing Identity Non-Aligned Sequence, and how she would very much like to know what that meant. She told Artan that the clinic gave them numbers, but that they gave each other names. She was Minas Flowers, her sisters all had names chosen from their dispositions and their preferences. She loved flowers. Pictures of them, flowers in the garden, she used to pick them, she used to paint them. She asked if Artan's mother had another name.

He hadn't even begun to process the fact that his mother had been a clone. The story Minas was telling him was just that — a story. He thought back to fond memories when he lived in a remote valley with his mother and father, their sheep and cows. He remembered the bees and how they buzzed round the trees. He remembered her companion bird. Crow, she called it. Crow would sit on her shoulder and eat from her hand. Crow would circle overhead, checking the land and, by its demeanour, reporting back. His mother and the crow were devoted to each other.

"Bird! My father called her Bird! Do you think that was her actual name? I thought it was his nickname for her."

Minas Flowers cast her mind back to a time when a gaggle of little children clustered round a window to watch the russet-coloured squirrels dash about the trees, and the birds would come and go, teasing each other and calling out. She could see in her mind's eye the squirrels and how they paused to pick up a nut or seed in their fine little fingers, and expertly open the casing, and nibble away the contents. She could see their impossibly clean white bibs and their twitching ears and their cheeky faces. One had a white tip to its tail, as if it had been accidentally dipped in paint. One of her sisters loved that squirrel with a passion and would hang for hours by the window hoping to spot it. She was Minas Squirrel.

But there was another, another girl who watched the trees, the one who cared for a bird. Its broken leg lovingly splinted, it's glossy black feathers iridescent in the sunlight. The bird who waited for her in the garden and would stay close whenever she was outside. They would talk, Minas and the bird. They had their own language.

"Yes, I remember Minas Bird. She loved all animals. She had a beautiful heart and cared for anyone or anything which was not well. A mouse, a fly, each of us. Minas Bird was soft hearted and somewhat strong willed." Minas

Flowers smiled as the recollection took shape in her memory. "We always enjoyed each other's company. We knew nothing else. Never a cross word despite the imprisonment. Tell me about her."

He paused to think back to a memory long buried. "The story is long and unpleasant. I did not have a chance to go back to my mother. Just like you, we were uncontrollably washed up on this beach maybe nine or ten years ago. I lose count. Adam keeps count. It's been a good life here. Enough to go round. The people already here made room for Blue and Adam and me, and we became one tribe, sort of. I have a daughter myself now, and a son. It's a pity Barwin did not live to see how well it all worked out."

He smiled to himself. He tried to pull away from the past, and failed. "There was an enormous hurricane. Almost as big as Angelo. Did you have it?"

"In New York? Maybe twenty years ago? Is that the one?"

Artan nodded.

"I didn't know it was that big. We were living in fear and dread at the time. Virus, hunger, storms and droughts. As bad as it gets. Yes, we called it Vincent. The only bigger storm was Angelo. That was a terrible year." And Minas too slipped back into a veiled past of half memories hidden in a forgotten corner of her mind.

"Judging by the wind direction, though it was hard to tell for sure of course, the valley we lived in would have been smashed to pieces, we always knew the risks, but sometimes you take them anyway. I would have gone back to find her, but our travels took us so far away, and to be honest we are still not sure of our exact location. She was with a caring man who would have looked after her had they survived. Our little boat was thrown and buffeted for days across the sea, and frankly we didn't much care about anything except being safe."

He paused, as if still trying to believe his luck. "Just look at this place. It is beautiful, it is simple. It is almost too good to be true, so we live the dream, always knowing that we cannot repeat the mistakes of the past. We, here, in this small and verdant place, will have the utmost respect for all living things."

Minas looked at him. "We had a son," she murmured. "A son. I did not even know it was possible. We should have been sterile. Maybe that's what our name implies. That we were a mistake. Maybe that's why we were imprisoned." There were a lot of maybes rushing round her head all at once.

Artan looked at her across the dying red of the fire, trying to rationalise the relationship. "Do you feel like my mother?"

She smiled that mysterious quizzical smile. "It is unexpected, but your whole story, thoughts of my sister, Bird, the warmth of the fire and a journey through life which has brought me here, to you, our son, maybe our only child, has me feeling a glow inside with which I am unfamiliar. A warmth born of belonging, for the first time since my sisters and I were separated I feel a bond."

For Artan, to learn that his mother had been a clone was a matter of deep interest. That he had been born at all was an accident of science, or maybe nature, or perhaps just a slip of the human hand. He was glad he had not had to worry about this before, because it was only natural that he would think twice whether or not to have his own children, had he known his origins he might have hesitated.

A young girl came bounding over, she was around ten years of age, brown skinned, leggy and healthy. A young chicken slept peacefully in the crook of one arm, and the girl smoothed its little feathers, lovingly, with the other.

"Minas," he said, for he could not quite call her mother, even though in a sense she was. "I want you to meet someone special. My daughter."

The little bronze haired girl looked up, the remaining glow of the fire flecking red in her big grey eyes, and Minas gasped in astonishment. "Oh my. Oh my. Oh my word. Oh…" She caught hold of herself so as not to upset the girl.

"She is. She really is. She is my granddaughter?"

Artan smiled. "I guess so." And he paused. "I wonder how many grandmothers she has?"

They laughed, a bittersweet moment shared, and Minas, looking into the dewy grey eyes of this child, knew she could not leave the island.

"What's your name?"

The girl looked searchingly into the older woman's eyes. "Minas."

"So is mine!"

Minas Flowers gently touched the child, then lay down exhausted. The Great Cosmic Lottery had brought her to journey's end. The abstract sense of longing which had blunted her existence flew on gossamer wings into the endless sky.

Chapter 12
Survival, Swidden and Forage

Ana lay on the sand, alone, soaking up the soft light from the sun. It was late afternoon and all the day's work around the homes and land was complete. The bay on which the *Constant Vigilance* was moored was wide and crescent shaped, on either end the sand gave way to boulder, then rock, then twisted out of sight to cliffs. The sand was occasionally broken by dark red rocks peering through the ground as if to see what was going on.

Vision made fuzzy by the sunlight, Ana imagined she could see a lone wolf standing on a distant rock, looking out to sea. He was healthy, his fur pale and thick, shining silvery in the low light of the sun. She thought again of Jake Dakotah. The wolf stretched his neck as if pointing out to sea, and he was still.

'Yes,' she thought to herself, 'I shall not stay long.' And the vision faded, as if its work was done.

Idris and Brita appeared and sat haphazardly beside her. Idris had wasted no time in bagging a tour of the island. Ana had accompanied him for some of the tour. They both needed to know about that most pressing of all needs, the food supply. Clean water was evident from their first landing on the beach, and although the island was sparsely populated, they were very curious to know how they nourished themselves.

Brita was Artan's bhean. She was a sturdy young woman of dark looks and easy smile. She explained in her beguilingly soft lilt that she was neither wife nor partner. Bhean was Gaelic for woman-wife, but there were no ceremonies, no ties, no legal piece of paper, just an acceptance from the community that these people were pairing for as long as they both wanted to.

She explained in a whispering musical breath of words. "Our little band of people were here before Artan, Blue and Adam came. We were leaving the mainland to get away from the death, the terrible death. I don't know why our beautiful Ireland was hit so hard, being rural for the most part. Some said it was the vaccines, that they were useless, some said it was our genetics. Some said it was an experiment which didn't work, for there was plenty of research going on and a dwindling population to try it out on. We set off in a boat. Heading for anywhere that wasn't Ireland. We weren't very good sailors and the currents had their own way with us, and we washed up here. Magical, isn't it."

Brita smiled, and smoothed her black hair back from her face revealing dark lashes around emerald eyes. She retained the classic look of the northern Celtic hunter gatherers, the eyes a lingering genetic trait born of isolation in the far west of Ireland. Strong, healthy and beautiful, she melded into the landscape as if fashioned out of the very fabric of the land.

"There were so few of our village left, and the memories, the pain and the suffering were no longer bearable. We were young enough to make a run for it. We took what we thought would be useful, seeds, potatoes, knives. We were like a bunch of newly recruited Scouts out on a sleepover." She laughed wryly. "Honestly it still feels as though we died and came to heaven — and then Artan and friends turned up, and we suddenly had a mix in the gene pool. We feel we are in the crucible of a new beginning."

"Do you have a plan?" asked Ana.

"Sort of. Mostly we've been making it up as we go along, you know, bending with the winds and the will of the island. It is almost as if it tells us what to do."

"I don't see any sheep or cattle," ventured Idris as he toyed mentally with his recently learned methodology for regreening.

"No, there weren't any here when we came, and we didn't bring any either. All we have in the way of domesticates are the descendants of Adam's chickens — just tiny little things newly hatched when they arrived. They are tame as can be, our pets who occasionally give eggs. We adore them."

"That's one reason for all these young trees. No grazers. You are lucky then. You started in a good place."

"To be sure we did," smiled Brita, and she looked softly at Artan who had just walked up to join them. "I was just telling Ana and Idris how fortunate we are to have found such a perfect place to live in."

Then, turning back to Ana and Idris, she said, "There is no explaining it. It was deserted. It was lush green. It has a microclimate which allows year-long growing, it is sheltered from the storms, there is fresh water, wild fruit, seafood. After a lifetime of barely surviving, all we can do it try and keep it the way we found it. I guess that's the lesson really."

The others nodded. That was indeed all which was required, to let it be. Ana and Idris had seen the low impact nature of food growing the Barwinians had adopted. The way they cleared just enough land for their needs, then moved every couple of years to let it revert to nature. The way they left the central swamp to its own devices; the way survival to them meant the survival of everything.

It was Idris, his recent studies finding words for their thoughts. "I guess, if we wanted to classify what you are doing here, you would be swidden agriculturalists and marine foragers."

The Barwinians nodded politely. They did not feel the need to classify themselves.

"How many people do you think the island could sustain without compromising your ideals?"

Brita looked thoughtful. "That'll be one of those tipping point questions for sure. How not to make the mistakes of the past? At what point do we stop having babies, stop welcoming visitors. At what point do we decide some must make the dangerous journey to another place."

The question remained unanswered.

"We'll know when we get there," suggested Artan. "The climate here may be super-stable for now, it might change. We just don't know. All we do know is that here, right now, there is a perfect balance of trees and shrubs, and swamp and water and insects, and room for us to carve out a little niche here and there."

"Another thing we will know for sure," added Brita, "is that our children will not understand the hardships we faced, and their outlook will be very different from ours. Goodness to god we hope they will never experience death on the scale we have witnessed, or starvation, or the massive upheaval in weather systems. All we can do is tell them about it, and warn against overshoot, against taking more from this island than it is prepared to give us. We are an invasive species here, and we had better remember that."

Ana was humbled. "I can only offer you homage. I am in complete awe of you and your way of life. Here you are far away from the struggles we witnessed in New York, heroic though their undertaking might be. For them the struggle has barely begun, for you it has ended. And yet… and yet… you may come to crave books and learning and art and history."

"We know." It was Artan speaking this time. "And those who crave it enough will be courageous enough to go and seek it. No one would stand in their way. Our duty here is to maintain the crucible in good and healthy order so that they may return to what they left. We teach only caring, kindness and co-operation."

Ana was enthused. "A new culture has been born here. I see it now. We will not stay long enough to truly understand it. We have our own destiny to follow, but please, stay in the light — by that I mean please, please always strive for higher meaning without compromising all that is good within you. I don't mean to preach, but history is littered with stories of once promising cultures descending into the kind of darkness which leads eventually to ruin. Greed, desperation, ambition — that sort of thing."

Artan and Brita glanced briefly at each other in mutual understanding. "We'll be on guard, but just because we leave a blueprint for the next generation, doesn't mean they will automatically follow it. We do not intend to be prescriptive."

Idris looked knowingly at his mother, Ana. "There always has to be room for expansion of the mind. The blueprint can never be finalised. I think Ana and I understand that. She encourages me to step beyond her sphere of knowledge, and that is both challenging and liberating. Your crucible cannot be a static device or you will stagnate."

They understood. "We have spent many years learning how best to physically survive. I see that developing a culture which will help us to cerebrally survive is at least as big a challenge."

In the back of his mind Artan was wrestling with the knowledge that his mother had been, or maybe still was, if you considered her clone sister as just another version of his mother, a clone. It was hopeless to conjecture what this might mean for his own children, in a genetic sense, or maybe even in a cultural sense. In a practical sense he imagined that he would know soon enough if they were fertile. It was a conundrum he was destined not to solve. When the visitors left he would talk to Brita about it, and maybe Minas too. It was sad that she knew so little about herself, but inevitable, for she was some kind of laboratory secret, a virtual lab rat. It was awful. He supposed that his greatest moral tussle was whether, and how, or even if, to tell the children.

"When are you lot thinking of moving then?"

The quiet conversation was thoroughly punctured by the rasping tones of Ishmael. He had been working on the boat for the past couple of days, accepting the odd bowl of food, but generally keeping clear of the islanders. The eternal suspicion that people who chose not to live on the sea were not altogether trustworthy, would remain firmly lodged in his psyche no matter how they might prove to him otherwise.

The group of four looked at him in unison, slightly startled. They were enjoying being away from the confines of the boat for a while. Clearly Ishmael had the opposite view, and he was the boss when it came to their journey.

Ana collected her thoughts, and a vision of the wolf briefly crossed her inner mind. "Well, I'm ready now. How about you Iddy?"

"Yep."

Ishmael nodded briskly. "The skinny one said she would be staying put. Fair enough, less for me to worry about — all that hanging off the bow in all manner or weather... Gave me the creeps I don't mind admitting. Shall we say tomorrow then?"

Chapter 13
High Pressure

Swift goodbyes were always the best, and the three remaining travellers climbed up onto the *Constant Vigilance* with armfuls of fresh fruit and vegetables. Small tokens were exchanged. Ana gave some sewing needles and fine thread — a much prized gift on an island which did not have either, and was unlikely to ever have either, not that she had anything much else to give. In return she accepted a little piece of finely woven cloth, made of berry-dyed feathers and coloured grasses which she assured them would soon be stitched into her skirt of generations.

Idris gave one of the precious books rescued from the New York libraries and, apart from the food, would accept nothing in return, the same went for Ishmael, who agonised over his gift for them and in the end decided some nylon twine might be the most useful.

Most of the little group of islanders came to see them off, the children, the chickens, Artan, Brita and Daisy Blue with her little girl Barwin.

Adam rustled through the small group with a woven bag across his shoulder. He walked into the sea.

"Do you think you could make room for me?"

"Strewth," muttered the skipper in mild exasperation. "We lighten up only to weigh back down again." He turned round to Ana and Idris. "That all right with you two?"

They welcomed him happily.

His partner Daisy Blue ran down to the water with her child and embraced him. "I know you have to go. I've always known you would take your chances when they came, but I've come to love you for all you have done for little Barwin and the island, and this is hard."

Little Barwin stood solemn, not understanding. Adam was the only father she knew, though biologically little could be further from the truth.

"Addy?" The child's confused face looked up into his. "Why are you going?"

He would never be able to explain adequately the reason. Life on the island had been happy enough, but for one omission, love. Earthly, mortal love. The closeness and companionship of a true partner.

Instead he took her lightly by the shoulders as she waded out to him. "Dear beautiful Bar, there are many different types of love, and I love you very much, and it's hard to leave you, but an important part of me is lonely. So I have to take this risk. Daisy Blue understands. It's a type of calling. This is the only boat we have seen in maybe ten years, there may never be another. Sometimes we have to face the unknown, and it's very hard."

The little girl started sobbing, uncomprehending, knowing only there was about to be an enormous loss.

The tears were streaming down Adam's face as he addressed Daisy Blue. "I have come to love you too, but we both know there is not enough for me here. I will take my chances wherever this boat is going."

Daisy Blue clutched him closely, and whispered into his neck, "You mended the broken thing which was me. I shall miss you like crazy, but I understand. Your heart needs to move onwards, and I'm glad a boat has eventually come to carry it."

He grasped Daisy Blue by the shoulders and looked her straight in the eyes. "You have been amazing. Friend of friends. You will always be in my mind for your kindness and understanding."

He picked up young Barwin, always like a daughter to him, and hugged her tight. Waved briefly to his friends and jumped up onto the boat.

Ishmael quickly untied it. "Let's get out of here quick before any more of you wretched land lubbers gets the same bloody idea."

With little more than a mild creak, the *Constant Vigilance* crept out of the shallow bay and into the swift ocean current which had deposited them a few days before. She turned southwards and rounded the dark cliffs. The beach became a flickering memory.

It took some hours before Ishmael could establish where exactly the island had been, and then he was not completely certain. He turned his maps this way and that, then put a dot in the ocean. Beside it he printed in beautiful copperplate handwriting 'Barwin'.

The sea was eerily quiet, frighteningly quiet, as if a great beast lay slumbering beneath them. The sailors each kept their fears to themselves, as if by giving voice to them, the very thing they feared would arise.

Flat, strangely flat, was the water, it felt as though the tides had ground to a halt, yet the westerly breeze skimmed the *Constant Vigilance* along the surface as if they barely touched it. It seemed that they flew. There was urgency in the motion and Ana felt that this swift and uninterrupted passage was a mercy gift, for she knew that the metal lodged in Hania's head was slowly blinding him, and he might not have long to live. Hours saved in travelling could be precious hours given to Idris and his father.

The water sped below them, silky smooth, the sky unfurled and for many days it seemed as though the boat sat still on a pantomime of brightest blue whilst the clouds rolled above them as if scenery unfurling from one longitude to another. They found their course and headed south, then east, and the Bay of Biscay slipped past unannounced, the ferocious old sea-dragon of storm and fury sound asleep.

"Best not go too close to land," said Ishmael as he navigated through the seven-mile space between Tangiers and the Isle of Tarifa. "They've 'ad it 'ard 'ere. Probably 'arder than anywhere. Last time I ventured through there were people swimming out from both sides. Terrible it was. I took a few on."

He shook his head from side to side in memory. "I expect you've 'eard what's 'appened. No rain. None. They are living — if you can call it living — on a prayer and that prayer is gettin' very thin."

Just a few miles into the Mediterranean, the boat slowed. Idris, Ana and Adam sat on deck in mournful silence as they surveyed the shoreline. No one was swimming out to the boat now. Either side was bleached and blackened. The crumbling old forts standing guard to nothing but pain and suffering.

"It looks bad," said Adam, shocked by the difference between the fertile island he had left and the barren condition of the land he could see. "But there must still be some places where life continues."

"Oh yeh, I've seen them 'aving a go. But the odds are against. When the aquifers are empty, the land burns away, and the rivers run dry, what can you do? There is a limit to how much it is worth desalinating when the food won't grow because of the heat. Too little change. Too late. Nothing but bad politics brought this on." And he clicked his teeth in bitter sadness.

The water below them changed from sparkling reflections of the infinite space above, to brackish melancholy. The Mediterranean Sea churned in hollow desperation as the too-warm water punished what life was left in it. It had been predicted, but it had all happened so quickly.

High pressure had sat over the entire Mediterranean basin for a decade. The gasping land had punished almost all life to an untimely death; the sea was forlorn and dying.

Feelings of gloom worked their way up from the sliming residue of a once fertile sea and seeped through the boat into the minds of the voyagers. The boat came to a sudden and uncompromising stop. Becalmed. The dread of every sailor.

"But we were here just a few years ago." Ana was almost disbelieving. "They were working hard to create new farm spaces in the cities. The countryside was impoverished, but people were surviving. How did it come to this?"

"Perfect storm really." He smiled at the irony of those words and corrected himself. "Ha! Or no storm at all. Bloody capitalists. Never wonder why I took to the sea and stayed there."

"Did you never think you should stay on the land and fight?"

Ishmael stopped what he was doing and looked right through her. "You think I didn't? Do you think I wasn't on the streets demanding system change? Do you think that any of us stood a chance against the billionaires? Nah. Waste of bloody time." And he began to tie knots in a length of rope in a particularly ferocious way.

As a sailor Ishmael had cause to study the currents, the weather, the jet streams and more. He calmed himself. "Not enough people were interested in stopping climate change, it 'appened slowly, so they did nothing about it. I guess the politicians couldn't make enough money out of it. Bastards.

"This sea. The Med. It's a particularly bad disaster area because the mountains all about stop the jet stream from bringing over moist air. Plus it's like a cesspool. It's got too warm. You need a decent difference between the land temperature and the water temperature for rain and a bit of wind. Looks like everything here just stuttered to a halt. It's worse than I dared imagine or I wouldn't have tried to bring you people here."

"Are we going to be stuck here?" Idris asked the question on everyone's mind. "For long?"

Ishmael clicked his tongue against his teeth. "High pressure."

The other three looked at him straight.

"Who knows. The biggest problem is going to be lack of food for a start. Just look at this water." And he gave the water a look of disgust.

"OK," said Ana summing it up simply. "So we're stuck here indefinitely, without much to eat or drink. We ration what we've got. We fish all day if necessary, because there must be something left in there." And she looked forlornly at the abysmal state of the water. "So come on people, lets prioritise. Ishmael?"

"OK boss. First we put out everything which can catch the wind, sheets, bedding, clothes, even that old skirt you're always fussing about Ana." He gave her a sidelong look as if to say the means always justified the end, so she had better not argue.

"Then stay as cool as we can. We'll rig up some extra desalinators using whatever we've got. We can fish out some of those plastic bottles still floating about and set them up in the sun. I'm going below to check out any radio signals. You never know what other mad people might be around."

Day and night blended into more days and nights. The *Constant Vigilance* barely moved. The amount of water they could distil was barely adequate, the catch reeled in was pitiful. A small Atlantic bonito, half a dozen anchovies and a sickly sea bass were all the catch of a couple of days with the net and line. Fortunately the produce from Barwin island would last a few days more, and longer life vegetables like potatoes and squash would last a while yet, even in this ninety-degree heat. The crew could only sit and wait it out. They studied the water, the sky the stars. They looked for birds or insects or any sign of life in the air and there was none. The signs were bad simply because there was no change in them.

In the second week a distant light shone from behind the *Constant Vigilance*. It was night, and up until that moment they had felt desperately alone. The light became stronger, larger, until it was a beaming sun glaring relentlessly on the four bodies trying to cool themselves on the starlit deck.

There was no choice but to make contact. Ishmael picked up the battered loud hailer. "Ahoy!"

Waves slapped at the side of the boat as the stranger came close. It was much bigger than the *Constant Vigilance*, more like a small naval craft, or maybe a coastguard. Patched and multicoloured it did not look official, though even the term official was somewhat outmoded in this panicky time of anarchy and survival.

"Ahoy!" came the response. "Do you need assistance?"

"Doesn't sound like pirates," muttered Ishmael under his breath. "But you never can tell." He put the hailer back to his mouth. "Can you take three extra on your vessel?"

"Pull alongside at the nets." Came the response.

Another light was switched on and pointed into the water where the storage nets were being lowered over the side of the boat.

Ishmael turned to the expectant faces of Ana and the others. "Are you game for going up on board? I'll stay here in case you need a quick retreat. You can jump off and I'll pick you up."

The three passengers looked at each other and nodded assent. Hanging round in this becalmed sea, waiting to die, was not much of an option.

"Come aboard."

The larger boat had swung round a few degrees, and in the upward reflection of light from the water they could see its name picked out in swirly writing: *Lucille*. It didn't look like a pirate, unless pirates were in the habit of adopting psychedelic hippy writing, but as Ishmael said, you could never tell.

Strong hands reached out over the rails to help them up the last few feet of the net and hauled them unceremoniously over the rails and onto the deck.

"Glad we found you. It's a bit tricky out there," said a plumpish man from inside a magnificent orange beard.

Ana straightened herself and regained her composure. "Well, who are you?"

From somewhere inside the beard a smile emanated. "We're what's left of the Rainbow Rebellion. We cruise up and down fairly regularly to pick up whoever is left. Gives us something to do."

Ana gathered a joke was implied and smiled at the friendly face. "We're on our way to Levanta — at least two of us are. The skipper of the *Constant Vigilance* has brought us from New York. It's been quite a journey."

The owner of the orange beard proffered his hand. "Hamish."

"Ana. Bit of a cliché with the beard and the Scottish name?"

He responded in a broad Scottish accent. "Not where I come from!" They grinned at each other, pooling good humour.

"Levanta eh? Why would you want to go there?"

"Have you been recently?"

"Always a difficult place. Bad history upon bad history. I have stayed away since the Abaddon. Reports have been terrible, awful. Disaster upon disaster. Why on earth do you want to go into these gates of hell?"

"It's personal. It's a promise to fulfil. We do not often have the luxury of true free will."

"On this ship we know that only too well."

Ana looked at him questioningly.

"We're all gay. We found each other in the terrible times when fascism was creeping into every country as the shortages started to hurt, and a few of us stuck together. Moving onto the ship was our most sensible move. We are not persecuted, we live our lives as we want, and the bonus is that we get to help people — like you. You could have been out there for weeks, the way things are with the changes in climate."

Adam and Idris were sitting close by under the shadow of a lifeboat strung above the deck. Adam smiled. Grinned would be a better word, from ear to ear. By chance he had found his people.

Chapter 14
Lucille

A murky dawn spread across the southern horizon, mingled with the bracken sky and the sandy dust lingering on the surface of the deck. The contrast between the putrid waters below and the open ocean they had left behind was upsetting, but as if to overcome the drab spectacle the *Lucille* was bedecked with makeshift masts and patchwork pink sails. The hull was a hundred shades of yellow — after all, paint was free, unlike food — and everything which could be painted was festooned and coloured with whatever came their way — plastic flowers, coloured bottles, ribbons and reflective garlands. If the *Lucille* had ever been battleship grey there was barely a trace.

The crew busied themselves about the ship. They were whistling and singing, happy to have visitors and to be of some use. They offered to give the *Constant Vigilance* a tow, but Ishmael, having more or less fulfilled the task of bringing his human cargo to their approximate destination, was anxious to leave this awful dirge of a sea and get back to something he recognised. Bundles of belongings were hoisted up to the larger vessel, bundles of survivable edibles were lowered down.

They waved and shouted their goodbyes to the old sea salt as he turned about to face the Straights of Gibraltar, sails hanging limply, current indiscernible.

Slowly the gap between them widened. The larger ship, under solar power in the absence of a breeze, made very modest progress, but it was at least progress, and Ana felt they were slipping silently behind an invisible curtain to a world of arid uncertainty. For the first time in her life she wasn't sure she was doing the right thing, but it was a promise, she reminded herself, so it could not be the wrong thing.

There was a party that night on board *Lucille*. There seemed to be many more people on board than she could have imagined. Men and women of all ages danced to the music of the good years, the old favourites, the disco and the schmaltz. Some had dressed up in feathers and spangles, they danced madly for hours as if there was no tomorrow, indeed the thought of tomorrow was a thought not worth having, instead, there was today, this moment, the very apex of existence in which they could be unfettered and free and laughing.

But Adam had found his tomorrow. He, and others like him had at first been free to live as their honest selves, then hunted down under the tyranny of fascist gangs and murderers. Cannibalism, had brushed too near. It was as if his life had unfolded in discrete segments, each new one shutting the door firmly on the old one, but the scars lingered. To be stranded on an island with lovely but abundantly heterosexual people was spiritually lonely. He wanted to love. He wanted to feel. The emotional solitude was killing him with the slow dagger of yearning. Yet without warning the very thing he sought literally appeared before his eyes as in a mirage or dream. He was still inclined to pinch himself, and he danced and sang with his happy tribe on the *Lucille* until the pale-yellow sun peered through the dusty dawn.

The tired waters of the Mediterranean grudgingly parted to let the old coastal patrol vessel creep through. Brushing close to the deserted Balearics, sitting squat on the water like slabs of blackened toast, many pairs of binoculars were trained on the shores and beyond, looking for signs of life, anything. Even a snake or a beetle would be a sign of life. From this angle at least, all looked abandoned. It was the same with Sardinia and Sicily. The land had become just too hot, too dry. Fires had raged until there was nothing left to burn. Any tentative green shoot would be fried by the sun and heat.

"It's like the end of times I always imagined," said Idris quietly. "All the little towns and villages are deserted, gone. We were here just a few years ago and I can hardly believe the change. I suppose the people died of heatstroke, or starvation, or just moved north… I feel I'm in a nightmare. Except the nightmare has already happened. Two nightmares running consecutively. The one I'm in and the other I'm witnessing."

Hamish was standing silently close by. "It all happened very quickly Id. No one wanted to believe the warnings. Governments as usual did nothing. Those tipping points so clearly pointed out to us by scientists suddenly accelerated the warming. People caught in the wet-bulb zones died in hours or days. They should have been warned of the dangers. The media didn't report very much because they were told not to alarm people. The media should take the blame for most of the deaths. If we had all known the truth we might have been able to do something about it. The exodus was over quite quickly really. Either you ran or you died. It's even worse where you are heading. You sure you don't want to change your mind?"

"I don't think we can change. We have to know. How could it be worse than this?"

"More warming, more war, and the Abaddon. It's hard to think of anything worse than that conglomeration."

"My father is there. At least the last we heard of him he was still there. Ana, my mother, promised that one day she would take me to meet him."

"She reckoned without climate change then."

"You don't know my mother. She knew plenty about climate change. She survived the first London flooding. Crisis is her element." Then tentatively, he asked, "Can you tell me about the Abaddon. I do know roughly, but I'd like to hear it from someone who might have first-hand information."

"Stories. Stories are all I have my friend. I was in North Africa on holiday. Madness. To take a holiday when the world is falling apart. I probably took it precisely because the world was falling apart. Last chance air flight and all that. I never made it back home. I've been in these parts ever since. No complaints."

"So tell me what you have heard?"

"Well, as I understand it, it was during one of those zoonotic pandemics, maybe the third or fourth. News was getting a bit sketchy. Propaganda was rife. Trust in government was non-existent. People were not turning up for work. Food was getting scarce. The only constant source of information we had was through the Chinese Internet, and then the translations were a bit dubious. Israel had developed yet another vaccine, and like some of the ones before, there was pressure to use it. People were dropping like flies."

Idris nodded. This checked with the story he had heard.

"I'm no virologist," said Hamish, "but it seems that either the vaccine had side effects, or the cocktail of vaccines in the body produced side effects, or maybe the virus itself interacted with the vaccine. I suppose that's a bit beside the point now. The real point was that the Israelis kept it to themselves. No sharing, you understand. Total exclusivity. Maybe they thought this was their key to world dominance? Maybe it was, for a while. In the years before the desperation of survival cut in there was still competition between nations for supremacy. It all looks so silly now."

He wandered off into his own past, down the rabbit hole of international politics, then brought himself abruptly back. "The long and the short of it was that Israeli women became sterile. No one noticed at first. Fewer people were having children anyway. Some Israelis had miscarriages. I guess it took a couple of years for the truth to simper out. I have no axe to grind either way, but the ongoing turf wars with their neighbours, the Palestinians, meant that an impoverished Palestinian who was not allowed to be vaccinated could have children, and wealthy Jews in the settlement down the road could not."

He shook his head in near disbelief, though everyone knew almost exactly the same story, "Can you imagine? The anguish, the retribution, the revenge killings, the slaughter, the suicides... That's why we stay clear of the place. Terrible. Of course, climate change is on course to kill us all, but that was an awful turn of events, as though all of the modern world's contradictions and stupidities concertinaed into one small space in time."

Idris layered this story on top of the others he had been told. There was little difference. He thanked Hamish for telling the blunt truth. "My father is going blind and could die soon. We need to get there as quickly as possible. Gaza is where he lives."

"Gaza?" exclaimed Hamish. "That was a putrid desert even before the worst of climate change. How does he survive?"

"I guess he's found a way. We're going to find out anyway."

Hamish looked over the rail to the barely moving water. "At this rate it could be a couple of weeks before we get there, and we have to make a stop in Cyprus first. See how our friends are doing there. See if we can load up provisions. We grow what we can on the ship. It's not always enough, but it does keep us in good shape." And he laughingly mocked himself by putting his hands on his hips to show off his less than small waistline.

Idris grinned. Hamish had a comforting attitude. The silver lining was never far away.

Someone waved them over to where a group was forming.

"They are trying to decide whether to call into Crete instead of Cyprus," said Ana to her son. "Usually they stop into Cyprus as there are a couple of communities there who are doing well and happy to trade, but as we are heading for Gaza there is a thought that it might be better, and more direct if we call into Crete instead."

The general consensus was to stick with Cyprus. Crete was too much of an unknown. The quartermaster's report indicated that it was time to replenish the stores. The lifeboats might be packed with salad crops, the hold full of mushrooms, but they had almost run out of wheat and barley, and everyone was looking forward to some Cypriot potatoes.

Hamish took Idris aside. "They took care of their forests on Cyprus, it was a wise investment."

Idris nodded. "How many people survived there?"

"Maybe ten per cent of the population. That's still a lot of mouths to feed."

"But they must have a surplus if they are trading."

"The question is, what will they trade for?"

Idris's mind started to tabulate possible tradeable commodities and apart from mugs and plates, pretty much drew a blank. "What would they trade for?"

"We're not so well stocked for tradeables these days, and we draw the line at ransacking museums and galleries — not that anyone wants a work of art right now. Almost everything we had in material terms has gone. What's left? Human capital, expertise, knowledge, slaves…"

Idris halted in mid thought. "Slaves? What?"

"We all want to survive. You work for food, for survival. Is that so bad?"

"I'm not sure that I'd want to survive at any cost."

"That's because you haven't yet had to make any of those choices, and maybe you'll get lucky and never have to. Pretty soon there will be new classes of people. Those who can organise successfully, and those who can't. How that develops in human hierarchical terms is anyone's guess. On Cyprus it's the forest dwellers who hold the cards. They keep the ecosystem alive. The ecosystem provides the microclimate, and that provides food. Cypriots see the value of the foresters, and the mountain people are organised. It might be different elsewhere."

"Meritocracy, kleptocracy, anarchy, slavery, wow, so quickly it can all form. Violence? Is there violence?"

"Probably."

'Yes probably,' thought Idris. He shuddered slightly. Levanta never looked particularly appealing in the first place, it was looking even less so now.

Ana had overheard some of the conversation. "We kept the lid on violence in New York City, but only just. And who knows for how long. One drop of rain, or its absence, will be the turning point. Attitude, cultural background, skills. They all play their part in forming the micro communities the world is breaking into. We'll be lucky to find one which suits us."

"And they are all subject to change. Nothing is certain, which is why we hold out on this boat. I'm surprised others have not had the same idea."

"Maybe they have. Maybe you're just the ones who got lucky."

Hamish grimaced. The crew of the *Lucille* always took precautions, they never let the mothership, as the *Lucille* was affectionately known, get close to shore. The lifeboats were useful for quick visits. They had a basic signalling scheme for ship to shore communications, and they never stayed away from 'mother' for a night. They had taken tough decisions and sometimes had to leave people behind. Between constant lookouts for desperate pirates who would raid and kill for the next meal and taking the risk to find that next meal for themselves, existence was always on the edge. Maybe they were the lucky ones. They had made it this far.

As the southern coast of Crete came into view, rising ashen out of the clouded water, they picked out a lone straggler in a tiny dingy. He or she was waving frantically.

"Uh-oh."

Ana looked at Hamish as he squinted through the binoculars. A few others joined him alongside the rails.

"Either a straggler, an escapee, or trouble."

"Plan for trouble," they said in unison.

Chapter 15
Death of a Dream

All attention was on the lone oarsman when a voice shouted out from the other side of the *Lucille*. Another, bigger boat had been spotted. They were sandwiched between the southern coast of Crete, the lone sailor and a bigger boat baring down on them.

"That boat is going faster than we could ever dream. What's powering it?" said Hamish mostly to himself, his engineering mind taking precedence over the need for caution. "Whatever it is, it looks useful."

"What's the playbook?" said the person standing next to him.

There was a general murmuring. The crew could be infected. It might be a trap. It could be pirates on the hunt for whatever they could get. The crew of the *Lucille* were not prone to fighting, but they would if they had to.

"Freedom or death," reminded another under his breath, reflecting the vow they had all taken, conveniently forgetting that actual events had shown that it was never that clear cut.

The ship drew nearer, and the *Lucille* ploughed her painstakingly laborious way forwards, for the moment ignoring the straggler in the rowing boat.

It was inevitable they would be outrun. The designated captain put the loudhailer to his mouth.

"Name your status," he shouted. It sounded about right. None of them knew any particular laws or rituals of the sea.

He waited until they got a bit nearer and tried again. Still no answer. He hollered again. "What is your status?"

Still no response. The larger boat was either unmanned or intent on foul play. It was bearing down on them at an acute angle.

"They are on course to ram us!"

"Bloody hell," muttered Hamish. "The only two seaworthy boats in the entire Med and they are about to collide with each other."

"Drop the lifeboats on the other side and swing her round!" came an urgent cry from the general consternation brewing on the deck.

"What about the lettuces?"

"We either get in with them or you empty them quickly."

"Looks like it's us or the salad. Give us five."

They lowered the small boats and started to gently take out the crops by means of the plastic sheeting underneath.

"We haven't got five minutes, get them out and get those boats in the water."

The gardeners looked forlorn. They jumped in on top of the months of painstakingly constructed compost, the beautiful bright green leaves, loved and cherished, crushed mercilessly under the scuffle of hasty boots.

Poles, broomsticks and whatever could be held out over the water attempted to stave off the upcoming collision, and the two vessels slowly ground their way into each other to the teeth-aching sound of scratching, scraping, gnawing metal upon metal. Above them could be seen a slouched figure over the wheel.

With no time to mourn, the remaining crew of the *Lucille* either threw themselves into the lifeboats or the sea, and the screeching, grating and clawing of one boat slowly devouring another continued relentlessly as the faster boat drove mercilessly forwards. The *Lucille* was at first carried sideways, then slowly, inexorably, bent into her painful death thrall, shuddering gallantly against the inevitable split, the deadly parting of back and front, fore and aft. Her hull loomed bright and yellow as it rose out of the water for a last sunny hurrah, pink sails waving their goodbyes and spreading like crinoline skirts across the water before being sucked back to the departing hull and diving to oblivion.

Those who could bear to look watched their darling, their mothership, their symbol of freedom, their brief encounter with honest joy, groan and moan and tear and slowly fade beneath the waves. A few lettuces floated to the top. A tomato bobbed back to the surface, but it was hardly hope.

Ana and Idris were floundering in the water as the buckled bow of the still moving aggressor ignored the sinking wreckage and passed between them and the crowded lifeboats. She loomed high. A rope was trailing into the water.

"Hang on!" yelled Ana, clutching at the rope and her son at the same time.

They clung tight, swept mercilessly towards land, lunging for survival, sinking and swimming, grasping at the rope, at each other, spinning and gasping, with no view to the land, no idea of how long they could hang on or when to let go.

Miles it seemed, interminable bouts of spluttering, half-drowning, dragging, banging against the ship and bouncing away. And then an undefinable noise. Grinding, from underneath, slowing, and the vessel shuddered. They looked at each other. "Rocks!"

"Let go!"

Sure enough clumps of shallow rocks were strewn untidily under the waters around the southern shores of the island. Boulders, the remains of coastal houses, the peeking blue dome of a seaside church. They half swam, half crawled across the debris, and clumped together, barely conscious on the baked ground. All that mattered was to recover a modicum of strength.

So this was Crete, or what was left of it. Heartbeats normalising, they sat up to survey their surroundings. Bare mountains all around. Bare, brown, dry rocks. Grey sometimes, bleached almost white in places, but not a whisper of green.

A couple of the lifeboats ground gently onto the shore — if such a broken and forlorn thing could be called a shore. People waded and tripped towards them, threw themselves down in dejection and sadness.

"I told you Crete was a bad idea!" Hamish had made it. Most of them had. They pulled the life rafts up on what had once been a tarmacked road. Some were anxious to find out what was left of the wreckage in the unmanned vessel, food and water being prime considerations.

A wooden boat rowed carefully towards them. The unmistakable Australian accent of the grinning oarsman shouted out, "Fat lot of rescuers you lot turned out to be!"

He got out and tethered the boat around a nearby road sign which crazily pointed to the long-submerged beach. The sign was brown and had a picture of a sandcastle on it in raised white contours.

"Here I am escaping some kind of chain gang round the other side of the island, and my first sign of help turns out to be a group of nutters who manage to destroy not one, but two seaworthy boats inside the first five minutes. "Strewth. You couldn't make it up. What a bunch of idiots."

Rueful introductions were made, and potted histories exchanged. The newcomer called himself Charlie. Nobody gave their real names anymore, there was no point. The less savoury characters changed their names with every new situation to avoid what they called 'complications'. It's not as if any of the remaining climate change survivors had a legal status, and it was not as if there was any legal machinery or government left to enforce such a thing. For some it was the chance to start all over, for others it was just a zombie mess peppered with a bit of hopium, as people were wont to call it.

Ana, recovering some strength, cast her eyes around the mountainous scenery.

"We seem to be at the bottom of a steep valley. There might be a stream, or at least some underground water. The ancient Greeks were pretty good with cistern technology. This place looks deserted. Probably they once grew a lot of food here. It will be worth trekking up that valley for signs of green, or bricks, or anything resembling a retaining wall." And she pointed due north.

A small group were returning from an early inspection of the shipwreck. "Pilot had an arrow in his back. Probably died at the wheel. A few bodies. Doesn't look like infection. Maybe attack, or mutiny. The good news is that they have a bit of food and desalination equipment. If we are quick we might salvage some diesel too."

They crew of the *Lucille* gathered round and decided their plan. They would make camp between the waterline, and a derelict area of broken glass which had once been greenhouses. Groups variously waded out and reclaimed food, liftable machinery, anything useful. Some would see if anything could be retrieved from the greenhouse areas.

Damage on the wreck would be assessed over the next two days. Lookouts, day and night were posted. Four people were not accounted for.

From time-to-time little bundles of random things bobbed towards the shore. One of them was a plastic package tied together with strips of old T-shirt.

"That's my skirt!" exclaimed Ana, wryly amused that her patchwork arrangement of memories had come to find her. It was vaguely heartening, as if her life was catching up with her and wanted more.

Ana and Idris busied themselves retrieving bedding and spreading it out to dry. They were both thinking the same thing. 'It's a long way from here to anywhere in a rowing boat.'

"We have choices I guess," muttered Ana as she wrung out a hand crocheted blanket of many colours. "All of them high risk and stupid. We could go north across land and try to island hop in a random boat we might possibly find."

"We could take a life raft and row the four hundred or so miles to Cyprus, and then, whatever..." Idris was laughing at the absurdity of it all.

Ana slumped down. "All with no food or water... I made a promise. But I can't do the impossible."

"Not like you," said Idris. "You like the impossible. It's a challenge."

"What I'd give for a cup of tea," she paused, momentarily reviewing the easy life of her youth, the times before hardship, flood and famine. It had all happened so fast. Had she known then what she knew now, she would not have been so happy to give birth to yet another life the beleaguered planet would try and support. Not that the planet had ever had any choice in the matter. Not that she had. The people who did have the choices, chose badly. The corporations, the bankers, the nameless and shameless — they knew what they were doing. The question was, where were they hiding now.

"Ah well, we only have one choice for the minute, and that's to muck in with this lot. One day at a time, as usual."

This was it. Every day a challenge for survival. People gave up, wilted away, watched their lives and their livelihoods melt to dust. Others fought for as long as they could, walked for hundreds of miles in search of a less hostile environment. Ana knew there had to be pockets of survivors somewhere on this island, hiding, coveting the few things they had, protecting their children, their goats maybe, their water supply. She felt pretty sure such groups would be inland now that the sea was dying. She suspected they might show violence to newcomers.

"Iddy, I'm going up that valley on my own. There might be people up there. I think there is a better chance of a non-violent reception as a loner. I'll be back by nightfall. If I'm not, don't look for me."

He obviously would look for her, but knew better than to argue.

She told the others and set off up the rough slope, following the lowest part, convinced that water once ran here, hoping there were still underground traces. Sticking to the shadows where she could find them, she was excited to be in a place where ancient history came alive. Ana had no practical knowledge, just the antiquated history books the old man kept on the creaking shelves in the Welsh longhouse. All a hazy dreamscape now. She wondered if the books were still there. As she clambered up the slope she wondered if the old place had been found by others. She hoped so. It was comforting to think of somebody digging into her vegetable patch, planting the seeds she had labelled and left stacked neatly in glass bottles. Wales seemed a good place in which to ride out and maybe even survive the end-times.

Picking her way round some bleached bones — goat, sheep, dog maybe, human also, young by the looks, older maybe as well. Scattered they were. She scanned the slopes of the valley. There were many bones. A pile of bones. More than she had first thought. Mostly human, though she was no expert there was something about human bones which could not look unfamiliar. It looked like a disaster scene. A mass dying event. Something had happened here which was not easily explainable. There were no signs of gunshot or other violent end. It was as if they had just dropped and died, maybe all at the same time.

She stopped to gather breath and turned away from the depressing scene to look back at the receding view. The barren hills either side of her giving way to steep sided valleys. Already the crew were tiny dots, the sea dull, with just the merest hint of sparkle from the dust bound haze of sun. She squinted into the distance, the blurry smudge where sky meets sea, and there was a single dark dot. It was crazy to think that another vessel could be coming their way — especially after so many weeks of seeing nothing. She looked for something to wave. Her shirt was practically the colour of the land, so not very useful. With a sudden sense of urgency she rushed back to the white bones, apologised to their deceased owners for disturbing them, and proceeded to spell out 'HELP' with the larger ones. Despite the burning sun she tidied them up a bit so that they looked purposeful and underlined the word with a scattering of little bones. It wasn't nearly big enough, but it was all she had.

Without warning the arid wind which had been blowing since they washed up on the beach dropped completely and Ana quickly broke into a heavy sweat. Inside five minutes she was wringing wet. Her face, her arms, her body. The thin clothes were already sticking to her. She was no longer evaporating to lower her body temperature. The sweat was running down her face, her chest, dripping off her buttocks. This was dangerous. She knew she needed to get to a cooler place immediately or she would die in a couple of hours. She didn't need a thermometer to know that the air temperature was suddenly more than the forty-two degrees prescribed as a limit to human endurance in high humidity, and the humidity was unquestionably rising. She knew millions had died from the so-called wet-bulb temperatures brought by heat domes and high humidity. Millions in almost every country between the tropics of Cancer and Capricorn and spreading north. In particular north. She panicked. She scrambled furiously down the mountainside, scraping her legs and hands. Below her people were already gathering in the water to lower their body temperature. The wave of humid air seemed to have come up from the sea. Everybody alive had knowledge of wet-bulb conditions and what action to take. When the wasteful energy infrastructure of earlier decades failed and air conditioning no longer worked, even the so-called developed countries had no defence from this. When the body overheats, brain haemorrhage and organ failure is inevitable. There was never a second chance.

Her head was throbbing. No second chance. Salt stung her eyes and she tried to blink it away. It was her own sweat falling like rivers from her forehead. Her vision lost clarity and she started to no longer care if she fell on the sharp stones or not. Crushing into her mind was the thought that this might have been what caused the death of those people on the hillside and she mustn't let it happen to her.

Scrambling downwards she dislodged a rectangular object. Possibly a brick or fashioned stone. She couldn't think why this was important. She was forgetting where she was or why she was there. The faded grey shape of a wolf flitted across her clouded eyes, and the sight of it was like a tiny shot of adrenaline into her bloodstream and she thought of Jake Dakotah and crawled a few more precious yards down the ravine. Slumping forward she felt a lifting sensation and was dragged into the sea. It felt cold and shocking. Her head was pulled back. Cool water was poured into her mouth. She passed from the brink of unconsciousness to consciousness.

"Boat," she croaked in a voice she did not recognise, and an arm flailed out towards the sea. "'Nother boat."

She stared back to the hillside to see the bony sign she had almost given her life to make. She could see nothing. The landscape was a bleached as the bones.

Idris cradled her, consternations written across his face. "Crikey Ana, you scared me to pieces. Thought you lost it there for a minute."

"Boat," signalled Ana. "Make them see us."

Chapter 16
Boat People

Idris helped haul her onto the flaking blue dome of a submerged church roof and she lay in the shallow water, strength slowly returning. "I'll go deeper when I'm sure you have attracted that boat."

People were gathering bedding and waving it around. They were scared about the heat and humidity combined and so took it in turns to leave the water. Ana could see the bright patchwork blanket pegged out on higher ground. There were no sticks or dried grasses with which to light a fire. Bedding would be sacrificed. Seaweed was gathered. The entire shoreline was a hive of manic people diving out of the water to complete a task then diving back again to keep their body temperature down.

The black speck on the horizon seemed to be larger. Ana kept her eyes fixed on it. It did appear to be heading straight for them. It was strangely unsatisfying. Friend or foe? Out of the frying pan and into the fire? Certain survival for a couple of days versus instant death?

The clamorous bobbing in and out of the water had slowed down. It was very likely they had been seen and the boat was coming towards them. They formed a circle in the water and talked. Ana overheard the anxious voices.

"If they wanted us to die they wouldn't bother to come here and kill us, they could just plough on past."

"They might be a raiding party, thinking we have something worth raiding."

"If we defend ourselves we might force them into combat which they may not intend."

"They probably want us for slaves. Who wants to be a slave?"

"I could do it for a while."

"Better then dying on this godforsaken rock."

There was a general mutter of agreement.

"OK, so we don't fight. We hope for a lift maybe. Where do we want to go?"

"Cyprus!" came the unanimous roar, and everyone laughed. There was a gay community on Cyprus, and the last time they called in there was food and drinking water. Put simply, there wasn't really anywhere else to go. Anywhere habitable that is.

"OK Cyprus it is. Slaves it might be. Death and injury to be avoided. How about you?"

"Gaza," said Idris. "We have to try for it."

"Maybe there is something on Levanta these people might want?" ventured Ana, clutching at the proverbial straws.

There was a general guffawing. "We don't mean to be rude, but the signs are not good."

"I know. So we have to change the signs."

Ana was returning to her element. "I have recent radio contact indicating exceptional breakthroughs in Levanta. We wouldn't be going otherwise."

She was bluffing of course. That was generally understood. But the plan was hatched, and the black speck once far out to sea took shape.

"Trawler," somebody said. "Though not much left to trawl."

"That's the trouble with trawlers. Killers more like. They killed the seabed long before the water heated. Bulldozers of the sea. Wreckers."

The bobbing heads in the water stretched their empty hands up into the air in submission and watched as the battered old workhorse came as close as she dared.

The hailer boomed out in a language they did not understand.

"English!" the group shouted back.

"You want ride?"

It sounded welcoming enough. They all shouted "Yea!" There was only trust. Anything else was pointless.

"One come close here for parley."

"You go Birdsey," suggested Hamish.

The assumed captain accepted the nods of his friends and swam out the few hundred yards to the trawler. A ladder was lowered over the side and he climbed up. Darkness was lingering around the horizon when a soft plop in the water announced his return journey.

The whole party gathered around the shore.

"Just another motley crew on the lookout for anything useful, a bit like us. There is a family on board. Little children. They are so beautiful. But it's a right old rust bucket. They were following the other boat in the hope of a better ride. I'm pretty sure they did not kill the bloke at the wheel."

"Where are they going?"

"Cyprus apparently. But they know less than us, just the word on the grapevine. They are really heartbroken about our little mishap. Two good boats lost at a stroke. Anyway, I don't know much but I think they are lost. Way off course. They started in Sicily I think. They speak that weird old Romance language nobody understands. Can't think how they survived this long."

"Can we all fit in?"

"No."

The old trawler was a mess. Practically held together by rust. Almost everything was broken on her. She had at one time been converted to LNG, then converted back to diesel. There was a forlorn attempt at sailcloth on the outriggers, and a vague noise coming from the general direction of the bilge pumps, but overall she was a dreadful sight and she didn't even have a name.

In the dawning light the disappointment was tangible.

"Silly old hopium. Always lets you down."

"Nah. It's good to split up for a bit. Both parties will have a better chance of survival. How many do you think she can take?"

"There's five on board. Two are little children, so maybe we should count that as four. She might take four or five more. Let's say four more." It was Birdsey — the assumed captain. He wasn't a captain and his name wasn't Birdsey, but he had a thick grey beard and a lot of experience of this particular sea. All the crew were happy to accord with his mild-mannered judgement.

There was a general shuffling in the pebbles as the inevitable choices were made.

"Iddy and Ana have to go on the boat. They are on a mission. They at least know where they are going. We… we are just hanging on, bodging about, hoping to stay alive for just a bit longer."

"Let's be practical. Take an engineer. That old thing might need some help now and then."

"I'll go," said Hamish. "I'd like to take Jonno if that's all right. We'd rather not be parted."

An Australian twang butted into the conversation. "I'd like to go along with you if that's a'right. I've been stuck on this bloody island for over a year. Could do with a change of scenery."

Everyone was happy with that. Hastily provisions were shared out between the two groups and the old trawler lugged herself round and headed in a general easterly direction, the children suspiciously eyeing up their new shipmates. The coast of Cyprus was more than four hundred nautical miles away.

"We'll be back for you!" shouted Hamish as he waved goodbye. "Just stay alive till then." And he and Jonno went back down to the bowels of the ship to watch over the flailing engine.

"Look out for ancient cisterns up the valley," shouted Ana as they left. "Steps going down. Some are underground. Look for masonry over bricks or stone walls. Bound to be a few around here. The Cretans were experts."

Chapter 17
The Trawler

"Life gets crazier," observed Idris to his mother.

"Well, we are heading in the right direction. And we are still alive, so all in all I think we are doing rather well."

He grinned. "Heading, shedding, spreading, bedding... Ha, ha, I know. You thought I'd grown out of it."

Ana grinned. Her son was an OK sort of person.

A small breeze fluttered in the makeshift sails. It was coming from the west. The tired old trawler chugged along falteringly. Hamish inspected the engines and came back with a blank look on his face which said everything they needed to know. The mother of the children was timid, but was glad to prepare a meal with Jonno. The recalcitrant skipper seemed to know roughly how to steer the boat. He spoke a little English and was apparently not the father of the children. Ana and Idris played with the older child who was about five years old, and was opening up nicely with little giggles at their pulled faces, whilst the younger, who was probably less than two years old, attempted to suckle at his mother but it was clear to see that she had little to give.

"Here we are then," said Ana trying to make light of the situation, "Moving imperceptibly from an unreasonable chance of survival to a marginal chance of survival. Sorry Iddy. I should have brought you earlier."

"You couldn't have known how quickly this all would have happened. I mean the Med disintegrating inside two years was not foreseeable by anyone. Those tipping points certainly tipped."

She smiled at him. He was still her son and she felt she had a duty to take care of him. Age was of course irrelevant. He was a man to all intents and purposes. He had the skills to survive.

"We could do with a bit of luck right now Id. We're still heading in the right direction, we just need to get there."

"Luck, ruck, muck, fuck... sorry Ana, that one just slipped out."

She ignored it.

They sat on the deck and looked towards the horizon, exhausted from everything, letting the slow yawl of the boat take their thoughts. "Might as well get some sleep — about three weeks' worth should do it."

The stars shone bright that night. The desert winds of sand and dust had blown themselves out and the air felt cleaner. Ana lay on the deck and watched the Milky Way turn slowly overhead on its great celestial wheel. Four hundred billion stars glistened above her. It was hard to imagine they moved at six hundred kilometres a second, so slowly did that awesome complexity of life, and planets and gasses revolve. The oldest stars were said to be as old as the universe itself. So much possibility, so much beauty. She breathed deeply and relaxed until she felt bodily attuned with the great cosmic order. How miniscule was her life when compared with this incredible stellar spectacle, how intellectually poor humans had all become. The Utopian potential had always been there, awe had always been there, beauty had always been there. She suddenly felt sick at the unravelling. All the learning, the technology, the art, the science and medicine, all reduced to a trembling foothold on life because of one simple misstep. No economy had been embedded in nature. The great economies of the world had been based on extracting something for nothing and now the bill was due.

The breeze had grown a little stronger. She pulled her patchwork skirt around her body for comfort. The tattered calico sails flustered about the rusted outriggers and seemed to be doing some work. Just a few humans on the road to who-knows-where. Just the empty sea, the Christmas sky, conserving energy, sleep.

A few peaceful hours later sudden brightness announced a perky dawn. Perky in a pink and yellow horizontally striped shiny kind of way.

Ana couldn't resist going up to the bow to catch this wondrous burst of brightness. Almost pure, almost clear. It was like a revelation, an omen, maybe something good or at least different. She smiled at herself. Already the possibility of hope was dancing before her and it wasn't the least bit scientific. She wondered if this was worth worrying about.

Hamish and Idris joined her, then Jonno and the rest. It was indeed a new dawn, and despite absolutely no sensible reasoning behind it, a feeling of wonder spread between the lonely mortals on this creaking ship and imbibed them with hope — for at least the foreseeable future — which was more or less the next day — which more or less illustrated how precarious life had become.

With the breeze behind them they were making decent speed, though it was impossible to tell how good. Most of the on-board instruments were broken or absent. At one time a well-equipped sailing vessel could cover a hundred miles in a day. The way this inland sea was behaving it could take a week. Hamish reasoned that turning off the engine might not be the best idea. It would save precious fuel, but he could not guarantee he could get it going again, and he figured that everything humanly possible should be done to keep them moving now that the wind was helping. Cyprus was about ten days away as the slug crawled, they had provisions for about six. Anything which speeded the journey time was good.

Every day dawned more beautiful than the one before. Sunrise saw them all on deck, religiously awaiting the moment, the minute, the microsecond of illuminating birth. Like the ancient pagans before them they waited, watching the horizon, only too easily imagining a slip into shamanism and voodoo. Desperate times begat desperate thinking. A myth was only an early science trying to explain an unpredictable world. A more advanced science had virtually destroyed it.

In the event the portents must have been good because they made it in five days without having to resort to mumbo jumbo and human sacrifice. The old ship more or less took itself into Paphos harbour, and a small welcoming committee stood ready to greet them, or at least to inspect them.

The people of Paphos looked bedraggled and tired. Once there would have been strict quarantine measures imposed, now it only mattered that you were still standing. The Paphosians were struggling, and it was difficult to work out who had been the most hopeful of respite — the boat people or the islanders.

It was clear they were disappointed that the boat was such a forlorn heap, but they gladly took the newcomers in, lavishing all the love they could on the children. A meeting was quickly organised. Places to stay allocated.

Ana had been quick to spot other boats moored in the harbour area. It looked very strange with only the top of Paphos castle peeping above the sea. The Ottomans had rebuilt it, the Turks had bombed it, earthquakes had cracked it, but the sea had finally claimed it. Everything which was once shoreline was now submerged. The new shore was car park, or promenade, or the exquisite Roman mosaics so painstakingly dusted clean from their burial of sand by a generation before.

Anxious not to dwell on Cyprus, Ana approached a woman standing near a small sailing boat. "My son and I are going to Gaza. Any chance you could take us there?"

The woman, young and blonde, unusual for these parts, answered in a strong American accent. "Why not," she drawled, a smile peeping through her carefully constructed dentistry. "Everyone is just sitting around here waiting to die, I might as well be doing something whilst I'm waiting to die. When do you want to leave?"

"Tomorrow?"

"See you around dawn."

Again that portent. Dawn. The smiling dawn of clear air and untroubled skies. Palest yellow tinged the blue of day and tickled the pinking hilltops to their east.

They left Hamish and Jonno to find a way back to Crete and help their friends. The Australian was happy enough to try his luck on Cyprus for a change. It was all the same to him. He'd lost everything. Family, house, children, friends. He was just drifting, waiting to die, and not understanding why he didn't.

There were boats, but not much in the way of supplies. They were advised to hop along the coast and find what they could. The north-west, where the forest came close to the shore, was likely to be the best spot, and others from Paphos were planning on going that way as life in the coastal town slowly disintegrated from sporadic shortages into one long shortage. The old were reluctant to move. The young eager. Calamities aside, the newcomers felt leaving quickly was right for both Paphos and them.

Chapter 18
Hania

He was sitting in a large underground room when the message was delivered. The room was furnished with sage green velvet curtains accompanied by old and somewhat shabby furniture of a classical design. The curtains were trimmed with gold tassels, a bit dusty, but still retaining a look of past days when there was space for elegance and charm. The armchairs were furnished in the same shade of green as the curtains, with abstract motifs of flowers and trees embroidered on them. Pictures stacked up along a cream-coloured wall, but they rested idly on the floor. None of them were hung. The frames were ornate and dull with a lifetime of dust clogging the intricate stucco design.

This was the old Ministry of Housing, now the Ministry for Ecology. Hania was its reluctant spokesperson. Around him were an assortment of men and women dressed in desert attire. Some wore the Arabic keffiyeh, others a Jewish tallit. Most disdained the continuation of such differences and wore the baggy shirts and dresses most suited to harsh sun and wind. The weathered faces of all present bore remarkable similarities to each other as they leaned into the middle of the carefully crafted olive wood table, still polished, from a tree a thousand years old, it was said. They leaned in to listen, because the spokesperson did not speak very loudly.

Although written in clear Arabic, Hania's eyes were too clouded to see it. He motioned for the messenger to read aloud.

"Your son and his mother are at the harbour in Gaza, and request a meeting."

Hania felt his throat tighten. When he spoke he realised the inner emotions could not be hidden. His voice cracked.

"Please, bring them to me urgently."

Hania leaned back in his chair. His hand on his jaw. It was the only chair with arms, not given to him for reasons of importance, but because it was easier for him to locate and sit in this type of chair.

He calculated the fifteen years since that chance meeting with a bright and energetic young woman on the long trail of refugees out of London. He smiled at the memory of her. They joked about all day, back then. He remembered the young doctors who never got the chance to operate on the shrapnel lodged in his brain. He could see all their faces. Bright, eager, thinking they had survived a great calamity. They had of course. The flooding of London had been shocking. It was difficult at the time to properly imagine the catastrophes yet to come.

Firenza was her name. All bright scarves and bushels of strong dark hair. He was immediately attracted to her vivacity. After a day or two it seemed the feeling was mutual and they gravitated towards each other right from the start. On the road, where camps were frequent and shelter scarce they made love every night. Beautiful, giving love, and rocked each other to sleep under the stars until they parted. They resolved to stay in touch and meet again when Hania had had his operation. He set out to find a hospital with the necessary equipment. She, determined to strike out on her dream to a verdant Wales, took a different road.

One by one the storms tore down the energy infrastructure. Piece by piece the channels of communication hesitated, then stuttered. They could have tried harder to find each other, but she was in a lost world of her choosing, an area too remote to contact, and he decided to go back home and help where he could before the metal in his head moved enough to blind both his eyes.

"Firenza." He whispered her name to himself, cocking his head to one side and smiling gently as only a gentle man could. She had told him about the boy, and he had rejoiced. She had told him she would bring him to Gaza when he was older, and so she had.

The others around the table studied his face in expectation of an explanation. He looked at them, eyes barely seeing. "My son is here," he offered. "Forgive me, but I will first attend to this wonderful moment. My friends, you need to attend to the swathes and plan for regeneration. We can meet and discuss the local composting tomorrow."

This quiet man who saw little but shadowy blurs, rose from the table with utmost elegance, and rested his hand on the arm of his brother.

"Let us go and meet them at the harbour, Chirag. And let us do it quickly before I am overcome with excitement."

Ana was fussing with her hair. It had not seen fresh water for months. For a woman who had always taken great care of her appearance, the tousled mass on her head was an abomination. Too long, too thick, too dry. It hadn't had to matter for the last few months, and she had been satisfied with a frayed ribbon and a pretty hair comb to keep the whole caboodle away from her face. Now she did at least want to look presentable. She combed it and plaited it, this way, that way. Tore it down, started again. The quiet woman who had shared the trawler with them motioned that she could help. Inside ten minutes Ana's brittle sun-baked hair looked as if she was straight out of a 1950's Hollywood glamour magazine. Ana beamed and thanked her.

"Iddy are you ready?"

Idris appeared looking exactly as he always did, tousled hair, rumpled T-shirt, shorts.

"Iddy, we are about to meet your father, we need to make an effort."

Idris hung his arms helplessly by his side. "I don't know what to do."

Ana had barely taken a brush to his hair when the Sicilian woman took it out of her hands and produced a pair of handsome hair cutting scissors.

'So that was her trade,' thought Ana, thinking further that there surely was a need for such skills in Levanta and noting to herself that she would make enquiries. Beauty in times of hardship did not need to be a luxury.

In just a few minutes Idris became a neater, tidier version of himself.

Ana shook out her patchwork skirt. It was rotting in places, but there amongst the fabric of memories was a piece of Hania. It was an embroidered piece of cotton handkerchief. He had lent it to her when she had a fit of the sneezes. She said she would wash it out and let him have it back. That never happened, and thus the corner of the handkerchief subtly announcing the letter H, or Ha, in Arabic, found its way into her skirt.

"OK. We're ready. This is it." She breathed deeply, nerves determined not to be quelled.

A pretty donkey pulling a colourful cart of red and white stepped gently along the harbour path. Ana knew this carried Hania. She sensed it. She felt faint. After all the months of travelling, the boats, the hardships and the waiting, she suddenly wasn't ready. The donkey was shadowing into a misty grey wolf. She pulled herself together. Yes, this was a big moment, but nothing she couldn't handle. Jake Dakotah was almost telling her, she pictured his voice, a deep resonant swirl of wholeness. She retrieved her confidence and smiled.

Idris held himself straight and whispered to his mother, "You only get one chance to make a first impression — at least that's what you always told me."

They smiled at the old adage, long forgotten.

Hania stepped lightly down from the cart, his brother standing by.

He smiled, his full lips curling kindly at the corners, and the eyes which could barely see light, watered silent tears of joy, and loss, and grief, and his face smiling and doubting and overcome, broke into little pieces of choking emotion, and he held out his arms. "My son…"

Ana guided Idris into those open arms, and the two men hugged, deeply, a long hug of timeless yearning.

The father ran his fingers gently over the contours of his son's face, seeking out the colour and character in the young bones and skin. He ran his hands deftly over the freshly tamed hair, noticing the sharpness in the ends.

"My son. You have had a haircut! Where do you get a haircut in these times? You must tell me if I need a haircut. How would I know unless you tell me! Maybe everyone needs a haircut, and they keep this important information from me." And they broke into nervous laughter, beginning the bonding. Wasting no time in making a connection.

Ana stood alone, sobbing, sniffing. Inconsolable happiness tearing her apart. It was a beginning and an end.

She had never questioned the future bond between father and son, and she had never imagined for one moment that these two hearts would not find joy in each other. It was a happy beginning coupled with the end of something wonderful — her joyful relationship with her son — and at the same time the herald of a lonely unknown, for her future was not to be here.

Hania took her hands in his. "Thank you dear Firenza. You have brought me the greatest gift possible. I do not know how you did it, how you got here and how to honour you."

She smiled and hugged him. "Your smiles are enough reward. But a nice plump bed would be a lot better!"

Again Hania laughed. "If there was only one bed in all Levanta, it would be yours!"

They walked and rode the short journey to the old Ministry and took the steps down to the basement. "This was the old government bomb shelter, sadly in almost constant use for more than seventy years. Now it is a cool place to sleep. We will make it nice for you, and you have the excellent benefit of a tap, and it yields water! Troglodyte living has many benefits as you will see."

Ana collapsed onto the makeshift metal bed already in the room. It had been a long and watery journey with little but uncertainty occupying her mind, and it had taken a toll. She had kept her promise and delivered her son, yet she had no sense of completion. Where sleep should have come, there was 'what next'. Her eyes would not close.

There was a knock at the door. A young woman came in holding a polished silver plate. On it was a single orange. For a moment Ana stared at it. She hadn't seen an orange for years. She thanked the woman and took the precious fruit. This was next. Of course it was. The orange was a symbol for the future. Something here was being made possible and her son might yet decide to be a part of it.

The following morning everyone at the Ministry shared a communal breakfast. Ana learned that Hania had lost most of his family to the incessant violence which had previously racked this land, his brother Chirag being his only remaining living relative. Of course a few hours ago that all changed.

Idris was anxious to know how they were greening the desert and was happily explaining the methods being used in the mid latitudes of America. He wanted to share what he had read about fungi, about the mycelium, plant communication and sustainability. He asked to be taken out to where this kind of activity was taking place in Levanta.

His father was anxious for Idris to see everything they were working on, and very keen to impart some of the joined-up philosophy they were working with.

"Idris. I see your mother calls you Iddy. I like that. May I call you Iddy as well?"

Idris nodded happily. He felt he was going to like his father.

Hania, who was in many ways in love with the philosophy they had developed, continued. "Iddy." He smiled at the familiarity inherent in the word. "There is a love we all share, deep within us. The love we need to show each other and the animals and plants around us. There is no love too great, no love too small, but an encompassing love for nature is, I think, the most precious love of all."

Ana paused in mid bite of the flatbread she was eating. She had heard words like this before — from Jake Dakotah. She congratulated herself for welcoming two such strong and compassionate men into her life.

Hania continued in his light but precise voice. "Only love can turn sand into a miracle. That is our great discovery. It is not about living or dying or personal existentialism or religion, it is about love.

"We have had almost a century of torment in this land. A broken and divided land. The people divided, the land divided, our hearts and minds divided. Everything from a pebble to a tree artificially divided. Such lamentable divisions brought a terrible outcome. These artificial divisions, all of which could have been healed, turned into an irreversible event. You know about it. Everyone does. We call it the Abaddon, and it will live on as a catastrophe even greater than our belligerent climate. When the vaccines were kept from our beleaguered people, malnourished, drought stricken, ill and dying, we believed it was the final nail in the coffin of Palestine. That our numbers would be so diminished from virus and malnutrition that we could no longer sustain our presence and the dominant tribe would trample our remnants to dust.

"But in the event, that was not to be the case. It was a self-inflicted wound and we Palestinians did not rejoice. I remember that we used to say our revenge would be the laughter of our children. But our beloved children were not laughing, for soon there would be no Israeli children to laugh back.

"It is difficult to understand how we absorbed this reality, and first we just sat quietly. If they must bomb us they must. But they did not. The shock was too great. This pivotal time was not without violence, perceived revenge killings, crimes of retribution, but both sides knew nothing could be achieved by it. Of course, the Jewish people might survive somewhere else, but here, on this arid land, they would not. They would die out in a generation. A long and unhappy generation."

Those round the table sat silent, for they knew more was to come. Even if they had heard it before, it was always worth hearing again. It centred them to think of a tragedy greater than the one they were living through.

"Resentment, of course, persists. On both sides. And the wailing of loss has barely subsided, but we have this common fight, this cantankerous climate, which is causing us to look beyond the past and make common cause. I do not know if this common cause could have been possible without the Abaddon.

"This land was already impoverished from overgrazing and mis-management. Drought and heat, humidity and hardship, death and dying looked to be the story for our children. Then everything started happening faster than even the most depressing scientists predicted. Climate change was suddenly our universal story, and we understood we could achieve so much more if we pushed with the work together. Great swathes have been cut through the hillsides and done fast because we could use smart and shiny Israeli machinery, and refined fuel had not completely run out. Time was at a premium. We imported most of our food back then, and overnight this stopped. There were catastrophic harvest failures in both hemispheres. Other countries needed to keep what little they had grown for their own people.

"People are still dying here. We cannot grow enough. We can only have more if we create more, and we can only create more in partnership. No borders, no barriers, one goal. And if we can achieve this, just think what we can do in other areas. All our hearts have to be in this work. We are recovering our neighbourliness, our community work, a new basis for co-existence, for food alone will not bind us together. That is why we have no Palestine, no Israel, no Lebanon, no Jordan. That is why we are Levanta, together, Levantines."

Ana finally replaced her bread on the plate. "That was beautiful, dear Hania, and such an enormous undertaking for one man."

"One blind man who could see what the seeing could not," said the quiet brother, Chirag. "There is a universal symmetry in that. The symmetry of blindness in those who will not see, being overcome by the person who cannot see."

"It was not me alone. There are many of us sharing this concept."

"And probably many more who could not see what you saw. It wasn't so easy was it." Ana was proffering a statement rather than a question.

Hania took her hand. Their short and crazy love affair had been sixteen years ago, but a residual fondness remained. "Dear Firenza, or should I call you Ana, you are right. It was not that easy. Some people carried lifelike robot dolls. Men and women. The desperation of harbouring a love for which there seemed no outlet was so great they named them, and took them around their friends, almost convincing themselves that they had a real baby. It was horrible to watch. And so we return again to the subject of love. There is enough love to go round. It just needs to be guided to a constructive place."

There was a murmur of agreement around the breakfast table.

"Of course resentment and sabotage persist in some places, especially in some of the older settlements. There

214

still exists a terrible anger. We risk being punished for being able to have children. Of course this is illogical — but no more illogical than being punished for being born here in the first place. Some have barricaded themselves in. We try to leave them food, but the risk of being shot is high. They seem to have a limitless supply of ammunition, but it will run out one day. We suspect the hardliners are preventing many from leaving those hilltop fortresses. The mistaken Zionist dream is over — at least for a couple of centuries."

Chapter 19
When Death Becomes Life

Hania was speaking to the people sitting close by. "Today we can attend to the composting projects." He turned back to Ana and Idris. "You are welcome to join us, but I insist on warning you that this is not a pretty sight. Our impoverished land yields nothing unless helped, and we have very little with which to help it. We are composting ourselves."

It was shocking and logical at the same time.

Ana was questioning the ethics and morality, whilst Idris looked fascinated. He could be described as being terminally curious — not unlike his mother. "Of course! Humans are water, blood and bone. Essential for plant growth. The heat will be helpful. I don't want to see any dead bodies, but I am interested in the process," he said with gusto.

"I'm in," said Ana, curious for different reasons.

Hania spoke so very clearly it was impossible not to mistake his meaning. "We, my generation, we know we can't make it, and maybe we shouldn't even try to make it through to old age. Many of us have even decided not to make it. Myself included — though I will postpone my own day to further enjoy this gift of a son." He looked fondly at Idris, a half-smile playing round his mouth. Idris shuffled a bit wondering where his existence stood in this complex web of life and death.

"Our only task is to make this place liveable for our children. When we have out run our usefulness, we must recognise that we have become a resource drain. It is a small sacrifice. We are doing nothing different from the woman who throws herself over the body of her child to protect it from bullets, or earthquake, or storm.

"Palestinians have for decades come to terms with their own death early in life. Malnutrition and violence have been our existence for generations. We expect not to have long lives. Now, at this stage of desperation, and nearly one hundred years of practice, we can see clearly that in order for the young to survive the old must give themselves. Not through overt suicide — though that is a viable choice for some — but through quietly fading, giving their food to make others healthy, their drink to slake another's thirst. It has been an easy choice for many. But it is not forced. We will do it now, just this one generation, so that never again will such measures be necessary."

"Well, the idea is not so bad of itself providing a person dies naturally. My jury is out regarding planned death," said Ana. "Who knows if this land will fare better than any other in the long run. Science is humble because it knows it is just a series of successive approximations.

217

There is no prediction. No absolute knowing the wind will blow this way or that."

They walked down the dusty track which led out to the long golden beaches, clean and inviting, unlike the grisly waters of the western Mediterranean.

"I thought the sea was dead," Ana observed. "But it's not, is it. It is just waiting to regenerate. Just a small pocket of life here, just a tiny eddy of health there. Maybe that is all it takes for balance to be restored. Looking at your shores, look at the sparkle. Maybe we have shrunk back from the ultimate tipping point."

"Who knows," said Idris. "A lot less people means a lot less harm, but not necessarily survival."

The little donkey followed the group along the sand strewn road, past the stubble of forgotten buildings, her head nodding happily, pulling her brightly painted cart. They walked on their own feet to rest hers, Hania's hand resting lightly on the arm of his brother, as always. When shade was found they stopped to cool a little, and when their destination was reached, the donkey was the first to be put under cover. The smell coming from the work in progress was not good.

"This was the sewerage plant. We obviously now need the nutrients for fertilizer. Everything used to be pumped out to sea. Now you can see the shore is clean, and the water clear." He chuckled. "At least that is what I am told. By the unpleasant smell I deduce things have not gone according to plan lately. We will have an explanation shortly I expect."

Indeed it seems things had not gone to plan. The balance for proper anaerobic breakdown of humanure had been momentarily lost.

"It's tricky," said the woman who stepped up quickly to explain. She spoke in hesitating English, which was the chosen common language. "It shouldn't smell at all. The received wisdom says to mix nitrogen rich straw and wood chippings in layers. We don't have a lot of either. We are improvising. We don't have a lot of worms either. Not yet, though there is a definite improvement on that side of things."

"So why does it smell so awful?" said Ana, who was very used to a composting toilet. The Welsh longhouse having nothing else.

"I think we allowed too much urine in with the solids. Maybe taking one shortcut too many. We'll bury this lot in the sand and come back to it in a couple of months when it has sorted itself out. In the meantime we must prepare the next load. There is no time to think about putting mistakes right. There is no time."

She left the visiting party in a flurry of floating scarves and flapping arm movements to supervise a cart load of buckets coming up from the town. Every household was tasked with separating their waste. Every bucketload was a means to survival.

"Now we go a couple of miles out of town to the other unit, and then we will look at the swathes. There is no midday meal for adults here, so I hope you can manage Ana. We have brought some bread for Idris."

Ana nodded. Going without was already a way of life.

"You may miss a few meals, but you will at least have a nice soft bed tonight."

Ana did fleetingly wonder if she was expected to share it.

They half rode and half walked to the hills beyond the shore. Here a breeze softened the heat of the day. Here the little donkey received water and scraps to eat.

They were on the border between what used to be Gaza and what used to be Israel. As they looked towards the sea, there were bombed out buildings and tiny fields of pitted ground. Behind them were the clear outlines of beautifully manicured, generously irrigated fields of a richer, once privileged construct. A construct which had a signature of waste and short-termism. A construct which might once have thought that it was above the natural order of things. But none of it had been restorative. Politically, humanitarianly, and agriculturally, the focus of this land of neat fields and barricaded settlements had focused on short-term wins, with the future being taught as something to fight for, rather than something to collaborate on. The space between the two land tracts was yards, the difference was almost horrifying, even now, a decade after the formation of Levanta.

"The lines are blurring now," said Hania. "We have paths crossing what used to be the border, and the field spaces are combining. The land is contaminated with the remains of old armaments, of course, but it's better than nothing. There's no time to be choosy. Come over here. I have something to show you."

Just beyond an undulation in the land, shielded from the sea, was a structure quite at odds with everything else they had seen. The arched entrance reminded Ana of Tibetan monasteries with its brightly painted reliefs of stylised trees and flowers in red and green and white.

"You recognise it?" said Hania to Ana.

"I do!" she exclaimed. "It's almost like a Tibetan monastery!"

"Ha!" said Hania delighted with her response. "This is you! You sowed the seed of this place in me."

Ana was nonplussed. It was almost incredible that her stories of Tibet, told round roadside fires in the aftermath of the London exodus, could have found a foothold in Hania's mind.

"I thought about you often. I thought about Buddhism, about sky burials, about compassion and exile. You painted these pictures in my mind, and when we started to plan a way forward for the dead and dying, long before famine became our paramount concern, when the ever-mutating virus ran viciously through our families and friends, we started to think in terms of mutuality. What was not Arabic and what was not Judaic. We changed the

221

symbols. We set to work constructing a simple place to nurse people through the last stages. Somewhere at peace. We had so little in the way of medicines, and obviously no vaccines, but we did manage to construct this. A beautiful sanctuary, where kindness and compassion could pave a gentle way to death and old divisions smoothed."

"But none of you are Buddhists!"

"Of course not. That's not really the point. We took a tranche of the philosophy for our own use and we did not even give it a name, just a place."

"I think the Buddha would be happy with that. I do remember how I would talk about building an invisible dome over Jerusalem. Protected from violence by Buddhist monks. A crazy girlish idea."

"Not so crazy. Your seed found fertile ground."

"As did yours," said Ana kindly.

"We made something good on both counts. We should congratulate ourselves!"

Idris looked away, abashed. He wasn't used to handling both parents at once.

They walked under the brightly coloured archway to the buildings beyond. Huts really. There were three, placed far apart. Inside the first, all was quiet colour and plump floor cushions. Paintings of nature and peaceful scenes adorned the walls. The second was not for visitors, for still they were trying to isolate and nurse the zoonotic virus cases. No one knew if these viruses were pandemic or epidemic, or just sporadic occurrences. They just were there, in the human population, and humans just existed alongside them. In truth the viruses had triumphed, for there was little left with which to fight them.

They were stepping inside the first hut. A burly man was carrying a wisp of a woman across the room. He set her down tenderly on some soft blankets and came up to the visitors. He introduced himself as Yossi. His English was bordering on terrible and his Arabic not a lot better. A translator hurried up to convert the Hebrew.

"I am so happy to see you. News has already reached us that this is the son of Hania. Excellent and beautiful news. We are all rejoicing. Welcome to the Village of the Passing. Here we watch over each other and our weakness transforms into strength. In this place of extreme generosity we dedicate ourselves to our children and the children yet to come."

There was a general array of smiles from around the room. Many were reposed on cushions, too weak to stand. Some seemed to be sleeping. Others were sitting on the rugs, talking in low voices, thin skin stretch over their faces and arms. It was a strange experience. No one seemed to be in pain. Some seemed very happy, euphoric even.

Yossi explained, "It is my gift in life to be able to look after these beautiful people, to ensure their comfort, to make sure they are kept clean and to administer little drops of liquid when needed. Some will be here for only a few days, others maybe weeks. It is all the same to me." His heavy featured face beamed at them, child-like, as if inviting a response.

Hania stepped in and bowed to the man. "My friend, you are a shining torch in the darkness. The gratitude of the whole of Levanta will not be enough to repay you for your work."

It was not appropriate to stay long, and they were guided out of the room towards the next building. Someone had been sent ahead to tell them to expect visitors.

"It's not perfect yet," said Hania. "But we are developing a system which is respectful and reasonably quick. It is not what I expected any minster of ecology to be helping with, but these are desperate times. We are trying to accelerate the breakdown process, but we have the same problem as earlier, insufficient raw materials such as woodchips. Once again we have to improvise. Let's go in."

A very strange mixture of greenhouse, plants and stacked shelves of closed metal cylinders greeted them.

"Not what you expected?" said the manager, all smiles, introducing herself as Fatima.

"No, not at all," said Ana, showing some obvious surprise.

"We try to make the process as dignified as we can — from every point of view. Oh if we had all the resources and time we would make this place truly beautiful. I have dreams and ideas for what it could be, but in truth we have to make this work as quickly as possible. Maybe one day I will have time to make my plans come real."

She led them across the sandy floor, past some raised beds of flowering plants. On one side was stretched clear polythene sheeting from halfway up the side to the apex, the other was a sturdy wall. "It gets very hot in here, but sheltered from winds and frosts and whatever the climate throws at us. We grow a few aromatic herbs, and of course healing and psychoactive herbs, for the sake of our humanity. The last journey should be paved with love and gentleness — and flowers. All year round we grow flowers."

Moving to the other side of the large room she gesticulated to some containers. They were round and made of corrugated metal, sealed at either end, about six feet long and three feet in diameter.

"These are the pods. They are just like rotary composters you would find in a garden. We rotate them every two days. You see nature knows how to transform our bodies into soil. Here we are just accelerating the process of natural decomposition."

"How long does it take?" asked Idris

"About thirty days if the temperature keeps up. As long as we have good bacterial activity and the right mix of carbon, oxygen, nitrogen and water. That is the difficult bit. We need to grow woody vegetation in order to utilise it here. Straw, woodchips and alfalfa, are ideal. It's a chicken and egg situation if you like. We need the compost to grow stuff, and the grown stuff to make compost."

"That is why we are taking such extraordinary steps to get ahead of the game," said Hania. "The virus caused countless deaths, and at the time we were deep in mourning and not planning for sudden and catastrophic shortages of food. We certainly had no conception that here on this deserted and barren strip of sand we would be desperately trying to grow enough to sustain ourselves."

Ana was jumping ahead. "Do you know if your process is good enough to kill all the pathogens?"

Fatima turned to look at Ana and said, with disarming honestly, "Frankly. No. We just know that we achieve over sixty degrees centigrade, and that should be enough. We have no sophisticated means of testing here. In the bigger cities they do have such equipment, but here we just have to work our plot of sand as well as we can, using the best of our scientists and knowledge."

Ana and Iddy thought it was impressive just the same.

Hania asked Fatima to take them round to the side of the building where the compost was collected and sieved.

Fatima pointed. "Most people do not really wish to come this side of the Village. On the other hand it would be quite all right if they came every day. Here is the compost material, you see how beautiful it is? We have separated the long bones for a separate process. They need to be broken down a bit more."

It was not possible for Ana to feel entirely comfortable with what she was finding, yet some aspects were very sensible. In a world of extreme scarcity, waste had to be a crime, and anyway, it occurred to her that the dead might be better suited to the earth than the living — at least if past performance was a measure of future performance. She smiled to herself, acknowledging the link she had made between human life and stock market jargon, a joke she thought best to keep to herself considering the situation they were in.

Fatima continued. "We know too little about soil function as a whole, the incredible complexity of ecological exchanges between plant and soil; the wonderful fungi, organic glues which stick it all together …" She was rushing to explain her subject, but paused for a moment to calm the carefree activity of some carts being loaded up, reminding the carriers of the need for respect. She continued. "But we do know that a healthy soil is our most important defence against climate volatility, and we are working with very marginal land and no dependable water supply. I believe we are making very good progress."

Hania's brother took the ensuing pause to mean they could now leave for the next part of their day's journey. Ushering his thanks, he guided the visiting party to a line of loaded carts just leaving.

Chapter 20
The Swathes

"You can walk or sit, or maybe take it in turns. The donkeys have much to carry, and their lives are at least as important as ours."

They walked gladly. Months at sea were not easily forgotten. The parched ground yielded softly under their feet and Ana wondered just how much in the way of nutrients had stayed locked up in the salty soil during the drought years. As they walked onwards, over the dune hills which shielded the inland regions from the shore, their eyes were drawn to a misty line between dune and sky in front of them.

"Nearly there. I can almost smell it," said Hania, a broad smile getting ever wider across his sun-drenched face. They were walking side by side and he took Ana's hand excitedly.

The visitors sniffed and stared. It could be that the mist they had first seen was hiding something greenish. They walked on, following the natural undulations of the land round some curvaceous outcrops of rock and stopped, almost in shock. For there in front of them, an exquisitely winding line of fertility, a stupendous concentration of life, stretched far into the distance, lavishing beauty and health across the verdant sides of a magnificent valley. It was green, unimaginably green, breathtakingly green. Tall green, short green, ground hugging green, bushy green, a huge and inviting desert spectacle of lush vegetation.

"This is what I really wanted you to see Ana," said Hania, kneading her hand absent-mindedly in his. "This is the stuff of dreams which come true. Ever since I can remember I have wanted to green this desert, this parched, desperate desert, and now it has been done I cannot see its greatest hour, but you can tell me. Ana, tell me what you see. I will believe you."

All the time they were walking further into Hania's dreaming garden. "I can see small trees, I can see birds, I can see shrubs and grass... and moss, and fruit, and... maybe running water... maybe a stream... and there's more. Across the valley are terraced fields, hundreds of them, maybe more... they are a million shades of green."

Tears were in Hania's eyes as he sought to see through the eyes of Ana. They sat down on a grassy bank, damp and fragrant. "Is it good? Is it happy? Is it working? Do you think it will survive?"

Ana linked her arm in his. "It goes on for miles Hani, right out of sight. The valley bends west and there is no break in the green. It must be dynamic because only an army of vast numbers could tend and water this, and there is hardly anyone in sight."

"I know," he said, staring with sightless eyes. "I can smell the moisture in the air. I can feel the spring in the

229

grass. This was a barren landscape when I first saw it, but I was convinced water once ran here. I knew the area had been deforested thousands of years ago, I knew we could do this. We created a myth, and the wonder is that so many people believed in it so many years ago. Ten years this has been in the making. Where is my son? Where is Iddy?"

"Right here, Dad." Idris somewhat shocked himself. The word 'Dad' just slipped in as if it was the most natural thing in the world.

Hania searched with his hands for the whereabouts of his son.

"Look, Iddy. We have water, we have birds, we have fields. This is what has been created from waste materials and ingenuity. That is why I showed you the other two places first, and once you start the process it becomes self-sustaining. We have created an ecosystem. It is sustainable. How resilient it will be is firmly in the lap of time, but as long as it is respected and loved, this could be here for hundreds of years — and it could even expand of its own accord."

Idris was impressed. He nodded his appreciation, forgetting that his father could not see.

"Iddy?" The father was searching for the approbation of the son.

"Oh yes! This is impressive. I think this is what they were trying to do in America. At least this is how it was explained to me. I'm not sure they succeeded, forever fighting the hurricanes and tornadoes and fires which plague that land."

Hania shook his head. "Maybe we didn't realise that in the end we were the lucky ones. Even the winds have changed and at times the rains have been coming back because of this restoration of vegetation, this little biosystem."

"Take too much out and it leads to desert, put it back in and you redress the balance — here at least — except the rest of the world is dying."

Hania shook his head. "Is it really dying Iddy? Or is it just marking time? I cannot save the rest of the world. I can only give them the methods we used. I will show you tomorrow. For now I feel suddenly very tired."

His quiet brother, forever standing by, helped Hania to his feet and supported him towards one of the now empty carts.

"I am sorry Iddy. You have found me at last, but this thing in my brain is moving, and I may not have so many days left."

Idris took his hand. "I'll stay by you. We can talk tomorrow."

Hania could not rest. "This terrible devastation of land and families has reunited us. Our tribes have been thrown together with each other and our people with nature. Maybe what we have in this novel ecosystem is unique. But we have to keep growing it beyond our own needs, and it barely meets our own needs as it is. One day we will abandon what's left of our cities and towns and plan a life within this new creation. We will need parameters. We will need guidelines. We will need to explore the philosophies of love beyond humans, beyond our own families. We can bring this love to other species of animals, even to trees and rocks and expanses of ocean. Truly, the human capacity for love knows no bounds. The sadness is that this love can be too easily tricked."

"It might be good not to reinvent the bible though, Dad. I bet that started out as some kind of history book with a life hacks chapter. I mean, if we have created the Garden of Eden through our own ingenuity, the accompanying manual had better not send out the wrong messages."

"Like — he shall have dominion over all the fish in the sea — and so on," said Ana, fearing that they had only just shaken off one era of patriarchy and could be grave danger of creating another even before the dust of hunger had settled. "That was a big mistake. The written word is unfortunately corruptible."

"Maybe we are destined to keep recreating the same mistakes." Idris sounded less hopeful than usual. Then a new idea struck him. "Maybe that's what humanity always does, unless we can break the cycle, you know, change the paradigm, maybe start in a different place and create a different cycle."

"How do we do this Iddy when the world is in a constant state of chaos and fluctuation? What is the point of Utopia if it has to be recreated again and again? How do we make men into mothers?" Hania was rambling a little. He was desperate to give his thoughts air, to share the entire contents of his mind with his son.

Idris tried to calm him. "Rest now, talk later. I'll stay by you even whilst you are asleep. We can talk again the minute you wake up."

Hania's voice was fading. "Iddy we have to find the key. The way to remember. People forget the hard times when they are enjoying the good times. The swallows did not come for years, then we changed something and they came again. People will forget the swallows stopped coming."

Three days passed with Hania slipping in and out of consciousness. Idris slept beside him, sat beside him, talked with him, soothed him, and only left for the briefest moments.

Chapter 21
The Children

On day four Hania felt better. "Refreshed," he said, and was ready to get up and back to work. This may have been the slow and imprecise meandering of the shrapnel in his brain, or possibly the body's reaction to the metal. Either way, Hania was not about to be stopped and no one was going to try and stop him. Idris was keen to explore the presence of mycorrhizal fungi in the swathes, but Hania was anxious to share other aspects of his dreamed future.

"Iddy, Ana, we have managed against the odds to tame the desert, and to just about feed ourselves. It is by no means a finished achievement. The planet has not stopped warming, there is a disaster waiting round every corner, and this we know, but there are other matters here in Levanta which are not yet overcome — that of the children, and their mothers, and their families. More importantly the matter of a lack of children for a quarter of our remaining population, and examining justice, and how best it can be served in a new world in a new paradigm."

Ana, Idris and Hania's team were taken just outside the city of Gaza where an old stone hospital had been repurposed into a children's village. As they walked inside little figures darted about squealing in delight in some game which seemed to offer endless surprises. A brightly clad woman walked briskly up to them and bowed to Hania.

"You have caught us in the middle of a great game. We are trying to find pieces of the world and put them back together again. There are some very clever hiding places!" She laughed gleefully. "I do not think it is in my power to stop this game!"

"This," said Hania, "is our esteemed and powerless leader of the Children's Society, Tova."

He stopped to let everyone introduce themselves, then said, "Tova has put together a model which attempts to share our precious children with the entire community. We can never place blame for the actions of governments on their citizens. It is not their fault they can no longer produce children, but in some cases there can be an opportunity to share some of the benefit, the love if you like."

Tova picked up the theme. "The state is answerable for much wrong, but now it is so much easier to move beyond the state when there is not a state to get in the way of your plans. This," she said, waving her hands grandly all about the six-sided entrance room, "is our children's village. It is an enabler, a resource, a hand reaching out, a community and an education centre all in one. It is of course a completely optional arrangement, and from time to time we review and update it, but here you can leave your children if you need to work, or just want a break, or simply because you like the arrangement and want to be part of it. You can arrange for them to stay overnight, you can be part of the helping and educating work, or you can just ignore the place completely!"

"Are you saying that these Arabic children are being looked after by Jewish helpers?" Ana got straight to the point as usual.

"Maybe at times this is the case, but we are all semitic, divisions along race are impossible. The only division here is that some have children and some do not, but those who do not can still be part of the wider family, plus there are those without children who never received the vaccinations, so you see this sort of arrangement can be quite levelling."

"Gosh this is tricky," said Ana. "How are people taking it? I mean, this is an entirely emotional situation."

Tova nodded. "We have to address this imbalance somehow. The important thing is that the children benefit from it."

As they were speaking there was a commotion coming from one of the side rooms. It was once the hospital waiting room, now a nursery for the very young.

"But I am her mother," came an insistent voice, getting louder and more tearful. "I am!"

Tova quickly went over to examine the situation. A younger member of staff was losing the ability to contain it. There was a small baby in the woman's arms, possibly only two months old.

"She is mine. Nobody loves her as much as I do." The woman held the child more closely. "I love her most. I do. I love her. She has to be mine. She has to be. She is. She is… she has to be…" And the woman's voice faded into a croaking whisper. She sank untidily to the floor, rocking the baby close to her body, sobbing pitifully.

Tova spoke very firmly, but there was nothing but kindness in her voice. "You are her mother in the afternoons, and I know how much you love her, but the baby stays here tonight."

The woman began to wail in Hebrew. "My poor empty body. Oh I am so empty. This is not a fair punishment. I am empty. My life is empty. Please let me take her home. I will love her more than anyone else possibly could."

Tova placed her hands on the woman's shaking shoulders, trying to still her. "You are full of love, and you are high on the list for adoption should there be an orphan. Your turn will come. I too am childless, but these babies all have families, and it is not their fault either. Be still now." And Tova took the baby, still sleeping, from the woman's arms.

Tova helped her up. "Come on, let's walk together, and talk, and see how we can mend this sorry world."

The woman complied, beaten, defeated, confused in her grief. They walked slowly out of the large entrance pillars, arms round each other's shoulders.

Ana was the first to speak. "Does this happen often?"

"Yes," said Hania, tears glistening around his eyes. "A terrible violence was done to her, and all her generation by the state. We cannot expect people not to respond to that. It's not as if civil disobedience or terrorism can change the trajectory of this tragedy of childlessness, but these are times of hardship on many levels. The response may be irrational and counterproductive, it may simply be resignation. Maybe it has taken her fifteen years to act. Every individual will respond in their own time frame."

"Will you let her back in?"

"Of course. She has done nothing wrong. She has simply acted from her own caring nature. This happens occasionally, but not as often as it used to. Sometimes we suggest very depressed people go out and work on the land. The four best doctors in the world are the sun, exercise, fresh air and rest. It is said that the smell of some microorganisms in the soil light up transmitters in the brain that release mood-lifting hormones."

"Yes," said Idris excitedly, who was not as affected by the recent scene as the others, and grasped at the opportunity to get back to his favourite subject. "It's the micobacterium vacii. It develops in the leaf mould and the compost. It helps release serotonin. I tell you the life in the soil is a miracle…"

Before his enthusiasm could get properly wound up, two girls of about ten years old bounced across the hall to them. "Auntie has asked us to show you round." There ensued a whirlwind tour of wall paintings, excited classrooms, tool libraries, books, and an array of ages all working together.

"We all decide how we want to be taught. Obviously we need to know the basic things like growing food and cleaning water."

"And building houses," chipped in the quieter of the two.

"And repairing things and cooking."

"And composting, and all that stuff, but we usually already know most of that."

"And do you live far from here?" asked Ana.

"Just a walk. Sometimes we live here as well. It depends."

"Depends on what?"

"It depends on our aunties. Sometimes we older children stay a while with them. It depends."

"Do you have many aunties?"

"A few. Almost everybody really."

Ana was burning with questions, and she was astonished at how naturally these girls were taking the novel arrangement. Obviously it was not particularly novel to them. The idea of collaborative childcare had been around for a century or more, and was, when you thought about it, the most natural way of bringing up children, multi-skilling them and socialising them. A flurry at the door heralded the reappearance of Tova.

"I'm glad you were here to see that. It's distressing, but it will focus your mind on the difficulties we still face.

The vaccines caused infertility because of a very short amino acid sequence in the spike protein of the virus which is partly shared with a protein in the ovaries. We made this awful discovery fifteen years ago. This means that we will be going through this trauma one way or another for the next thirty years, and we have to learn to deal with it."

"What lessons have you learned Tova?"

"Projects, activity, creativity, responsibility, exercise, planting, growing things. It's far from relentless, but right from the beginning, when the state collapsed, there has been plenty for every individual to do. Anarchy can be a beautiful thing when people are left to organise their own communities in their own way. We have hundreds of small communities, all learning from each other. Hundreds of children's villages. First they were a reaction to the absolute necessity of caring for orphans, then the equally absolute necessity to work for the land. It was later that we saw they could be used as a tool for cohesion, for therapy, an outlet for love."

Ana nodded in appreciation of the statement. "That's what everyone has discovered. Small numbers can self-organise. I guess that's what the viruses did for us. Cut the numbers into manageable proportions." She paused and thought of New York, briefly wondering how it was working out when there were thousands of mouths to feed.

"Hania and I have put our heads together over this many times. We are always planning for the future, for contingencies, for wobbles. We can't plan for every disaster. We only just made it past the last one!"

Wry smiles played round everyone's faces. No one really wanted to think about disasters, though in truth they were thinking about the next one all the time.

Hania put his arm round the shoulders of Idris. "On the way back I will tell you about our plans. We must leave Tova to her work."

The donkey walked at a slow and steady pace, ears flicking this way and that, half listening to the conversation, half thinking about home, and food, as donkeys do. Behind her Hania explained to Idris how they would gradually move out of the tired and crumbling cities into the green swathes of the agricultural land.

"To be near our food supply and for everyone to understand it, how it is grown, how the land is fed and so on. We have plans which I will show you. Seed banks, repair shops, spaces for innovation and invention, animal sanctuaries, eco buildings. Everything carefully thought out, and with the children at the centre of it all. It's become our overriding purpose now that the swathes are established."

Ana looked at the two of them. Heads together. Father and son. So balanced, so alike, so in tune. It had been worth the journey just to stand back and watch them in this precious minute.

A man strolled unhurriedly up to the cart. He was struggling to look calm, hands in pockets, but a wild look in his eyes. Chirag registered the look too late. Accustomed to being very close to his blinded brother, he had lately stood back to allow him intimate time with his son. They had years to catch up on and he knew how anxious Hania was to tell Idris everything on his mind. He could see how carefully Idris listened. Chirag judged they needed as much space together as was possible.

Too late Chirag registered the likely meaning of that wild-eyed look. Too late he realised that Idris could never have known what was likely to result from it. Too late Chirag lunged the few paces forward to intercept what was to come.

The man addressed Hania in impatient tones and came almost close enough to touch him. "Why wouldn't you give her the baby when she needed it so badly. Why? Tell me why? She just killed herself because of it. You killed her." And he made a stabbing movement towards Hania's body with his right arm.

Hania looked carefully at the man, unseeing, surprise on his face. His side was bleeding. "My friend, I am so sorry to hear this. We would never have wished this sadness on you. It was not her fault, or mine or yours. I am so sorry."

He slumped, holding his hand to his side as the man withdrew the knife, bloody, tears in his eyes, Chirag diving between them, a nanosecond too late. Not in years had he dropped his watchful eyes over this beloved brother. Idris gasped in shock and stood up to strike the man in anger.

"Leave him Iddy, stay with me a while."

He bent over his father, helping him to lay across the wooden seat. "Dad?"

Hania winced as Chirag applied pressure to the wound. "Ah," he moaned. "I was not very far from the end in any case. I think I'm a little nearer now. Iddy come close."

Idris put his face close his father's. Stroking Hania's cheek, seeing only that he was in danger of losing the coveted thing he had only just found.

"Iddy, closer. I think I can see your face." The dying man smiled and ruffled this son's dark brown hair. "You look like me! All brown hairy head and my father's nose!"

He tried to chuckle. One hand stroking his son's adolescent cheek. "So many things I wanted to tell you. Little things, silly things. Life things. I have written many of them down in case you could not find me in this human mess. Chirag will give you the book of my messages to you." His voice trailed off. Blood was spreading across his abdomen, soaking into his white homespun robes. Big red blotches seeping ever outwards, a dam bursting, a life draining, transfixing, horrifying.

"Can't you help him?" choked Idris to no one in particular, knowing in his heart that there was little to be done. Resisting the facts. Knowing only the absolute desperation of the moment.

"Iddy." The voice was fainter. The hand fell from his son's cheek. "Iddy. It would be nice if you stayed here and helped make our plans work. You'd be an asset."

Idris didn't even know how to think about this.

"No deathbed promises required…" Hania attempted a wink and a smile. "I think I have done enough here… Ask dear Chirag to plant a tree with me. Thank everybody. I did not leave time to thank them all…"

He lay, concentrating his mind deep into the eyes of his son, seeing him for the first and last time, even as Idris's grieving tears dropped onto his face, salty, hot, confused, angry.

"Dad…" The only word. The word he had only had three chances to use in his entire life. "Dad… Don't go now… Dad… Dad…" he repeated, struggling to smooth his father's greying hair under the fallen white scarf.

His father had already gone.

Chapter 22
The Reasons

The weeks passed. The sun rose a little earlier every day and the cycle of life and death continued in better balance than it once had. The recent rage of highly mutated virus had subsided. The frantic activity of previous years was giving way to a pattern of life, and little by little the fashioned stones from deserted buildings were carried to their new home in the swathes, and the process of moving materials and memories from the site of old histories to a site where new histories and memories would begin. It was slow careful work and would take years. They hoped they had decades, but in the meantime tent villages were developed along the planning lines of Hania's original intentions. Tents today, leafy boulevards tomorrow.

The trials of Hania's forlorn killer had been concluded. Restorative justice being the only type of justice conceivable in this emergent community of survivors. Born as they were from a system of retribution and heartache, they wanted something better for their children. The man had been tasked with naming his own punishment, and the community had been tasked with agreeing or disagreeing. The debate could continue for days until there was consensus between the offender and his community. Most of the proceedings had been done in silence, with hand signals for agreeing or disagreeing. In this way there could be no bullying, no justice of the mob, no shouting or abuse. The death of Hania, who was largely revered as the architect of their survival, had angered many, even though it was common knowledge that he was unlikely to live much longer because of his injury. That he should die in violence had inflicted pain on them all, and not everyone was forgiving. Restraint and patience were the only requirements for this process of justice, and the facilitators had been gentle but firm. Speech was only useful for clarification. In this case the man had chosen to spend the rest of his life working with the composters, and the community had agreed.

The philosophy of universal welcome was also debated and refined. All were welcome, the proviso being that each would have to earn their stay according to their energies and attributes. It was unlikely that they would be overrun with too many people because there were not too many people left to do the overrunning, but they would be needing more people to help sustain their population, to compensate for the childless ones.

Hania's tree was planted in the centre of the new plans close to what would one day be the Centre for Collaborative Childcare. It was an olive tree. Hardy, long lived and nourishing, it was an iconic tree of the Middle East and a sturdy survivor. Olive trees could live over a thousand years, and it was therefore a fitting memorial. Its potential lifespan would probably outlive the collective memories of how the new communities begun. The pioneering group agonised over what to call this, their first intentional community, to be built from scratch, or at least from the stony remnants of older towns, from the earth, from the palm leaf thatch they could grow and the bricks they would make. It was inevitably sustainable because the steelworks no longer produced steel, the cement factories likewise were defunct. Every pioneering community would use the building materials closest to hand, learning from each other, helping each other, building with each other.

The visceral joy and sense of achievement from building your own dwelling from only the land you stood upon was tangible. The work was joyful. There was little in the way of ready expertise, so trial and error became the principal teacher. Some structures didn't last too long, but they were confident they would eventually find the best methods. Building from the land was to become one of the basic codes of living the new life.

Debates raged as to what to call their first community. It was important to them to get this right. What language would be appropriate? Should they name it after a person, a thing, a tree? In the end Ana suggested they use a neutral language with no local historical root. Thus the new community simply became known as 'Morehu', the Māori word for 'Survival'. The concept was by no means guaranteed, but hope was a great motivator, and it became common practice to name new communities with positive nouns. To that end there were communities called 'Bliss' and 'Celebrate' and 'Delight'. There was one unspoken unwritten rule — that no community would bear the name of any previous entity or person. The tragic history of warring factions would not be allowed to interfere with social progress.

Organising, envisioning and applying the ideas to reality as it was on the ground was Ana's strength. The vision for a new way of living had ironically been conceived by a man who was blind. He envisaged what others could not see. Hania could feel what was needed and had not been swayed by exterior concerns or historical patterns. Ana helped organise the future towards their shared goals — that everyone on the planet would have an equal amount of comfort and wealth and political power. Ana, like Hania and the others, firmly believed in the politics of place, of geography, of culture. The quality of everyday life, local accountability, the relationship with the swathes in the hinterland and people who chose to live on the periphery.

A pretty grey butterfly with four red dots on its wings landed on Ana's fingers as she was sitting on the grassy slopes of one of the swathes. It was an Apollo butterfly, once on the brink of extinction.

She looked gently at it. "It is a miracle she has survived. If we don't have any serious setbacks, this place could be an island of sanity for all living things."

Idris examined the insect. "Sanity born from the womb of horror. It was not the primary intention though, was it? We were selfishly trying to save ourselves."

"The law of unintended consequences perhaps? I guess that giant web of life hasn't given up on us completely."

Ana hummed a familiar song to the butterfly as it perched on her index finger. The tune was pretty, almost a lullaby. It was the song she had first heard in England a seeming lifetime ago. She had sung it many times to Idris when he was a baby. They heard it again in New York. It had become an anthem for their hopes, their prayers, to 'Let the children sing again, Let the grass grow high, Let the people live again, under the starlit sky'.

Idris smiled. He recalled the song and how it had become almost a prayer for hope back in the darkest days after the tornado in New York. "I might be being too hopeful, but I think we can get it right this time, but like Dad said, the important thing is not to forget."

"You know, Iddy, at one time it was easier to imagine the end of the world than to imagine the end of capitalism. Now capitalism has ended I can hardly imagine the end of the world. But aside from inventing another religion, which we definitely do not want to do, I am having trouble with anything resembling a rule book, no matter what nebulous terms might be used."

"I remember that discussion about teaching men to be mothers."

Ana hummed the old song again, a smile on her face, head raised slightly to the sky. "That's where we should start Id. From the sowing of the first little seed, men can be mothers, or at least foster mothers. Midwives too. It should start with the earth and end with the earth. There were once moves to make violation of the earth a crime. They called it ecocide. It was never codified into law because the pollution industries fought against it. In any case it would probably have been too late. Yes, in order not to forget, there must be a simple way to remember, not just written laws, but songs and plays and events, games too."

Idris nodded encouragingly. "I like it. Let's put some ideas down."

Little by little the new codes were debated, deconstructed, simplified, reconstructed and agreed. They were called 'The Reasons' and were neatly transcribed by hand, illustrated and beautified, then passed out to their neighbouring communities for them to use if they wished. It was a beginning of sorts. It was their way of remembering.

Everything is done for the next generation
The spirit of sharing all resources never fades
Love and respect for the land and all living things
keeps us healthy in mind and body
All building materials will come directly from the land
on which we stand

Every decision will be made through equal gender collaboration
Space for wild animals will always be available
Agriculture will be regenerative and organic
Good is what's good for the biosphere
Art and beauty are forever our sustenance

"It's quite a long way from the Ten Commandments," Ana joked as she and Idris were out one day, walking the pathways between the swathes for some respite from the forever meetings.

"That's because there are only nine of them," joked Idris, lifting the corner of the very first geo-textile he had laid to encourage the magical mycorrhizal fungi growth and stability. "At least it might prevent any more Flood stories creeping into the vernacular."

They laughed together, mother and son in light-hearted mood now that most of the substantial planning work had been completed.

"Indeed. I've lived through one of them, and sea level rise is certainly a flood story for many. But you do get the feeling that all this has happened before. That each time we fail to sustain our garden, our cosmic niche, each time we forget the incredible complexity of ecological exchanges, we somehow get another chance to do it better next time."

Idris weighed the proposition carefully. He was sixteen now. An adult by any reasonable measure. From

Ana's perspective he was metamorphosising spontaneously from child to trusted friend. "Maybe this is the last chance we have, but in some ways, it is easier now. There are so few of us left to sustain."

Ana cast her eye lovingly around the valley, the beautiful, lush swathes of fertility stretching out around her, the outrageous experiment which had worked. "Morehu can feed five hundred people all year round, but no more. Some of the other communities can feed less. There will be pressures in the future to feed more, of that I am certain."

"That future might come, but for my lifetime at least we will have a decreasing population."

Ana nodded, it was impossible to forget that up to half of all the women she met were infertile. Impossible to forget how Hania had died.

"Ana," Idris took a more serious note. "I know you will eventually move on, but I think I am going to stay. It's not because Hania asked me to. It's because I like it here. I like the people. I like what they are doing, and I know I can be useful."

A cloud which had been building overhead caught her attention and the butterfly flew away as the breeze cooled in the changing thermals. Above her in white and silvery grey bloomed the shape of a crouching wolf, gathering himself from among the random pillows of vapour, outlined in white light against the translucent sky.

"I'm glad, Iddy, really glad. Bringing you here was difficult, but in doing so we fulfilled more than the sum of our expectations. Yes, I can move on with a clear heart and mind. You will do much good here, we both know that. Before I go, I have just got one thing to finish."

In her cool basement room Ana had been painting a huge mural on the wall. It was the story of her son's life, of his birth and their journeys together. The Nine Reasons were woven carefully into the story. There was only one last thing to add — the symbolic passing of Hania's life to Idris.

There would be new stories to tell round the evening meals, no doubt new myths would arise, but this, this gift from mother to son, would preserve at least one truth in bright and vibrant colour — that if you look for it, everything in the end becomes a beautiful symmetry.

"Where will you go?"

"North. To the lands I have never stepped on, the air I've never breathed."

To be continued…